the house on everly lane

LAYNE DEEMER

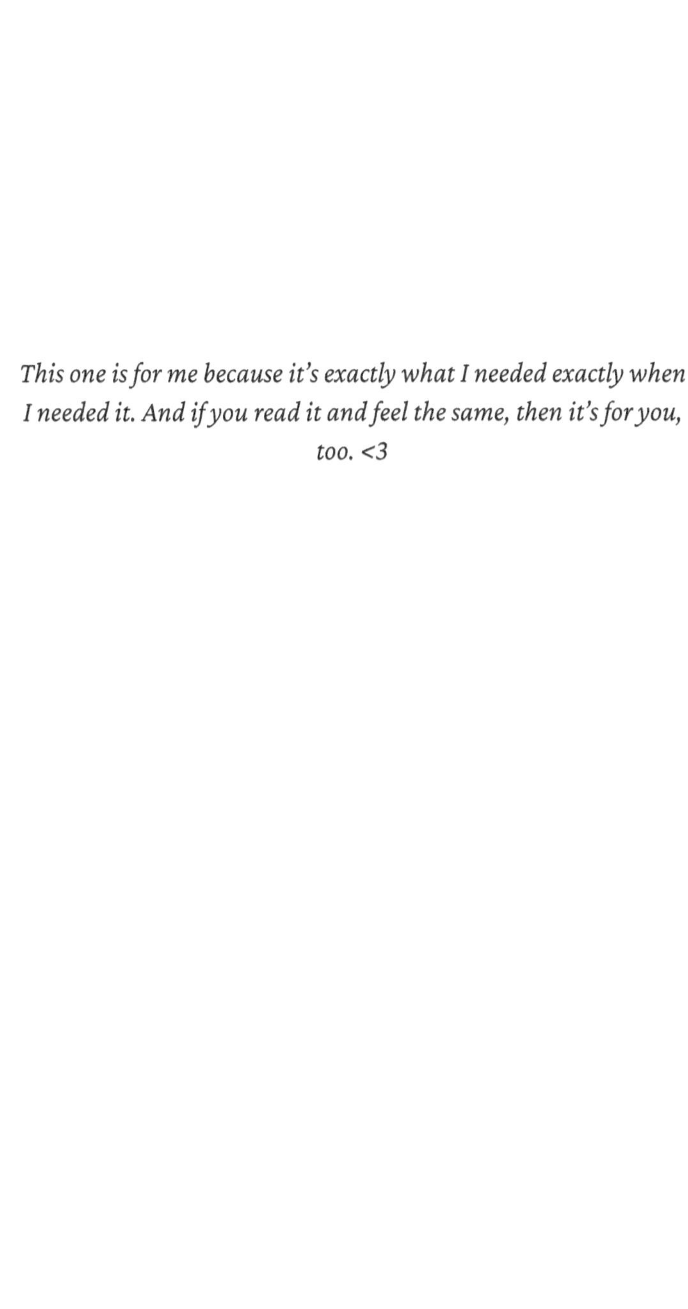

This one is for me because it's exactly what I needed exactly when I needed it. And if you read it and feel the same, then it's for you, too. <3

The House on Everly Lane was previously offered on Kindle Vella.

Please note, due to adult content, my books are recommended for readers age 18 or older.

For a detailed list of content/trigger warnings, please visit my website: www.laynedeemer.com.

Thank you!

one

DARCY

My eyes flick between the slip of paper in my hand and the gorgeous little cottage in front of me. It looked adorable in the pictures, but in person, it's indescribable—like something out of a fairy tale. I must have the wrong place, but, no, the ad said Everly Lane. Plus, the number I wrote down coincides with the number on the house. A copper plate is affixed over the front door. The wooden number 1634, painted in a pale blue, is mounted on top. Even the house number is adorable.

The front door opens, and a petite woman with drawn-on eyebrows and cherry red cheeks juts her head outside. "Darcy? Is that you?"

"Hi!" I wave. "Yes, I'm Darcy."

"Well, don't just stand there. Come on inside."

I take a few tentative steps up the front walkway before stopping a few feet from the door. "Mrs. Fitz, right? We spoke on the phone."

She frowns. "Yes. Haven't we already exchanged pleasantries?"

Not at all. She said my name, and now I'm saying hers. It's more just stating the obvious. There's nothing inherently pleasant about it. But from the severe set of her dark penciled-in eyebrows, I don't think she's a woman that takes kindly to being challenged.

I give her a small smile and continue walking. Instead of moving aside for me to pass, she shoves the door wide open and leans against the frame, forcing me to squeeze past her. I try to make myself as small as I can, but my elbow brushes against her chest, and she huffs.

We stand in the vestibule, and I can hardly contain my excitement as I take in my surroundings. The listing said the house was fully furnished, but I assumed that meant only the basics, like a sofa and maybe an end table. It's been my experience that furnished places available for rent give you what you need and only what you need. Once again, this home is proving me wrong.

It's small but open. Just from my vantage point alone, I can see the living room, kitchen, and small dining room. One flows right into the other. The living room has a stone fireplace with a live edge mantle. There are a few small geodes and a set of tarnished candlesticks with pale blue taper candles resting on top. A large flat-screen TV is mounted above the fireplace. A cushy gray sofa sits in the center of the room. It's the kind that makes you want to sink into it with a book and a glass of wine. It's bookended by two simple yet beautiful walnut end tables. Each one has a matching lamp, the same shade of blue as the taper candles. The walls are a muted gray—a color that seems to continue throughout the house. A small table with four intentionally mismatched chairs sits in the dining room, positioned below a barn beam light fixture. Several pieces of artwork adorn the walls in both rooms. The place is meticulous and should be featured in a magazine.

I look over at Mrs. Fitz and find her studying me with the same sort of scrutiny I used while looking at the house. Although from the set of her mouth and the narrowing of her eyes, I'm not so sure she's as enthralled with me as I am with this place.

"Your hair." She sniffs. "Is it natural?"

I run a hand through the copper mass, lifting a few strands. "It is. A little gift from my mom." I smile; she doesn't.

"Hmm," she leans in. "And you have a wire running through your nose, too." She makes a tsk sound with her tongue.

I tap my nose, probing the ring in my left nostril. It feels like she's making a list of pros and cons and only finding cons—at least, according to her.

"Um." I clear my throat. "This home is lovely."

"Yes, it is," she agrees, but her nose scrunches like she's smelling shit. "I'm afraid you're going to have to show yourself around. My knees aren't what they used to be." She waddles into the living room and plops onto the sofa. "I'll be here if you have any questions."

She's certainly not the most welcoming person, but if she's okay with me checking the place out, I must still have a shot. I stroll from room to room, admiring the large windows that allow natural light to filter in.

Upstairs, I find two bedrooms and a bathroom. The bedrooms are just as cute as the rest of the house, with impeccable decor. One is slightly larger, with a bay window and a built-in bench. Is this place for real?

I step back into the hall and notice a door at the very end. Gripping the handle, I start to twist.

"That door is off-limits!" Mrs. Fitz's voice booms behind me. I spin around and find her only a foot away, glaring at me.

Holding my hands up in front of me, I offer an apologetic smile, but it's met with disdain. "Oh, I'm sorry. I didn't realize. I was just giving myself a tour—"

"It's all right. I didn't mean to yell." She pauses, working her jaw back and forth as though the pseudo apology tastes rotten on her tongue. "This is my daughter's house. Karen. She worked hard to make it perfect, but then Ralph came along and well—he wanted to try living in Hawaii." She rolls her eyes and shakes her head. "So now they live there and I'm stuck here tryin' like hell to rent this place. Up there," she motions toward the forbidden door, "is where they stored the things they weren't able to take with them."

This house is full of not only furniture but decorations as well. It seems to me there's plenty they left behind. The idea that there's more upstairs—things that are "off-limits" — intrigues me. I'm keeping that to myself, though. I'm already doubting whether or not I made the cut with Mrs. Fitz. If she thinks I might snoop around, she'll never rent to me.

"Now," Mrs. Fitz claps, jolting me to attention, "do you have any questions, dear?" I'm momentarily stunned by the affirmation. It almost sounded like she meant it, too.

"Um, well, I love the house and am grateful for the opportunity to see it. I guess my only question would be, when do you think you might come to a decision?"

Her lips twist. "There's nothing for me to decide. That's up to you."

"Oh! I just assumed you had a lineup of potential tenants."

She laughs, a full belly guffaw complete with a knee slap. "Honey, this is Baker Hill. It ain't like I have unlimited options. You want it? It's yours."

My eyes widen. "Wow, really?"

"Yes, really," she says with an impatient tongue.

She hobbles down the stairs, her short form slowly disappearing as she descends.

I race to catch up with her, surprised at how nimble she is despite her misgivings about her older body. "When can I move in?"

"The sooner the better," she calls over her shoulder.

We spend the next ten minutes going over details that boil down to a verbal agreement that I won't play my music too loud or have any wild parties. It seems Mrs. Fitz equates body jewelry with unruly behavior. I shrug it off. She told me she and her husband live across the street. They'll learn soon enough that I'm more of a curl up with a good book and lights out at ten kind of girl.

She hands me a key, and when I offer to write her a check for two months' rent, she waves me off. "There's no need for that. Just push a check through my mail slot each month. I don't even care what day, so long as it's within the month."

"Do you want me to sign anything or do you need my driver's license?"

"Is there something I should know about you?" She squints at me with sharp eyes.

My mind drifts to my ex-boyfriend Chris and the humiliation he caused. It's partly why I'm here in this town to begin with. And something tells me Mrs. Fitz wouldn't approve if she knew the mess I've left behind. Luckily, she doesn't strike me as the Googling type, so I think my secret is safe for now. Hopefully forever. "Nope." I grin. "With me, what you see is what you get and what you get is a quiet girl who's more interested in reading than anything else."

She hums through pursed lips. "Well, then, Darcy—what did you say your last name was?"

I didn't and I still can't believe she agreed to rent to someone without references, let alone knowing their full name. "It's Simon. Darcy Simon."

"Okay, Darcy Simon. It's nice to meet you. I'm Ella and my husband is Bill, though you won't see him much. He's a bit of a couch potato." She holds a hand up to her mouth and whispers, "That's code for lazy shit."

I chuckle, and she smiles, finally. It meets her eyes, making them crinkle on the sides. It's amazing how much a smile can transform a person's face. Hers softens every harsh line, every sharp edge, making her appear almost grandmotherly.

"Where did you say you were working, dear?" She clasps her hands at her chest and leans in.

I smile wide. "Baker Hill Library. I'm the new children's librarian."

She hums, drumming her fingers on her chin. "That's right. Milly told me the last girl was leaving. My Karen always loved her books, too. Until that miserable Ralph came along." She tips her head, looking up at me. "When do you start?"

"Monday," I say with a slight grimace. It's already Saturday which doesn't give me much time to prepare, but the head librarian assured me the children's section is in excellent shape. She called it "move in ready," whatever that means.

"Well," Mrs. Fitz says, clapping her hands, "I guess I'll

leave you to it. If you need any help moving, I can give you the name of a guy from church."

"I actually don't have much and what I have, I think I can manage."

She nods, looking around as though she's trying to commit the place to memory. Maybe she's taking a mental picture of the "before" so she has something to compare to the "after" once I'm gone.

She's halfway out the front door when she pauses, looking back at me over her shoulder. "This place has been vacant for far too long. It'll be nice to have some life in it again."

I watch the woman, small in stature but not in attitude, as she stalks across the street. Just as she ascends her porch, she turns, casting an odd look up at the home she just rented to me. I can't quite tell if it's concern for the house's well-being or lingering sadness from missing her daughter, but whatever the reason, she has nothing to fear from me. She seems to have some preconceived notions about people with nose piercings, but this girl keeps her nose firmly pressed between the pages of books.

Once Mrs. Fitz closes her front door, I dash outside to retrieve my suitcase from the car. I meant it when I told her I didn't have much of my own to move in. There wasn't much time for packing, and besides, what little I left behind, I can replace. It's the people I'll miss the most. Which reminds me, I told my mom I'd call once I'm settled.

Plucking my phone out of my pocket, I swipe it open, but before I can make the call, a dull *thud* startles me.

two

DARCY

It came from upstairs—the forbidden attic. I chew at my lip as I try to talk myself out of investigating the sound. Maybe one of Mrs. Fitz's daughter's boxes tumbled over. But what would make that happen? Oh, no. Don't tell me there's a mouse.

I shiver, peering up at the plaster ceiling. What are the chances I'm not alone in this house? It's been vacant for a while. The odds are pretty stacked against me.

Just then, I hear the faint sound of scratching. I imagine tiny claws scraping at the walls in the attic. I groan. I can't just ignore it.

Maybe Mrs. Fitz knows someone who could come and take a look. An exterminator or someone less afraid of tiny things on four legs. But as I reach for the knob on the front door, I stop myself. I am here in this house because I ran away. Sure, things at home weren't very welcoming, but still, I didn't even bother trying to fight. When the shit hit the fan, I bolted. Now here I am, ready to do it again.

I groan. "Why am I choosing now to go all 'independent woman' and suddenly face my fears?"

Turning on my heel, I trudge up the stairs and to the door at the end of the hall. On a deep exhale, I twist the knob and tug the door open. A set of wooden stairs greets me, and immediately, I notice they aren't rough and pieced together like the attic stairs in my parents' home. These are smooth wood that have been well cared for. They have a slight sheen and a rubber tread on each step. The railing is a deep, rich walnut that gleams from the hallway light pouring in.

As I tiptoe up the stairs, the wood pops and creaks with each step. If there *is* a mouse up here, my chances of finding it are pretty slim now.

Once the room comes fully into view, I gasp. It's a library—the likes of which I've never seen. Rows upon rows of books adorn a multitude of shelves. Each one labeled with letters of the alphabet.

The ceiling narrows at each end and the shelves follow the curve. They've been carefully crafted for the space out of cherry wood that makes the room feel warm. Light filters in through large skylights, bathing the room in warmth. It's perfection.

"Mrs. Fitz, I think we may have a problem. Now that I know this exists, I'm never going to be able to stay away," I mutter, running my finger along the spines. I lean in to read a few titles and am impressed with the variety. I spy a leather-bound edition of the *Complete Works of Shakespeare* —no surprise there. Nestled next to it is a hardcover of *Bram Stoker's Dracula*. A few shelves over, a weather-worn dust jacket catches my eye. Moving closer, I squint at the letters on the spine. Stephen King's *It*. I pluck it off the shelf, careful not to mar the delicate paper cover. The image on the front is iconic—a storm drain with green claws reaching from the depths and a little paper boat floating nearby. When I peel back the cover, I'm stunned to see Stephen King's sharpie signature. Another turn of the page confirms it's a first edition. "What is this place?" I marvel.

* * *

JEREMY

She's only been in the room for a few minutes, but I already have her memorized. I didn't have to work that hard. There's something familiar about her. Something just out of reach. Or maybe it's just that she's the first younger person I've seen in … I don't even know how long it's been. Months or possibly years.

Her eyes gleam as she takes in the expansive collection. She likes it here. I heard her say something to that effect, but it wasn't necessary. I can tell just by the way she moves around the space like she's holding her breath. It's not unlike a child creeping down the stairs on Christmas morning, staring in wonderment at the wide array of presents under the tree.

She hasn't noticed me yet, though I'm not sure she will. No one ever has. It's strange sharing this space with her. I've grown accustomed to being up here undisturbed. Alone.

Her mouth rounds as she spots something on one of the shelves. With a raised finger, she glides a book from its spot. Grasping it in both hands, her eyes flit around the room. I would hold my breath if I could, but I haven't had air in my lungs for as long as I've been up here. I'm not even sure I have lungs. There's a moment, a fraction of a second, where I'm certain she sees me. It's as though her eyes trip the moment they land on mine, and once they've regained their footing, they're moving again as though they hadn't ever stumbled. I could be imagining it, but I hope I'm not.

She takes her book of choice over to the tufted wing-back chair in the corner. Tucking a leg underneath her, she sits down and smooths her hands over the turquoise velvet. The chair looks soft and inviting. I should know, considering I spend an obscene amount of time on it, but I can only surmise the way it feels. My sense of touch left me the moment my heart stopped beating. Memories are all that remain and even those are few and fragmented.

She clears her throat, and it's as if time stops. I crane my neck, peering around the stacks. She stares intently at the pages, but it's her mouth that attracts my attention. She sucks in her lower lip, nibbling on it. I don't think she's aware of the habit, but right now, it's all I'm aware of. It's endearing and completely adorable.

My eyes dance over her features and pause on the ring in her nose. It's new. I'm not sure how I know that. It's not as though it's out of place. It suits her. I just wasn't expecting it, is all.

The sun picks that moment to send a ray through the skylight directly over her head. It casts a glowing aura around her. Her copper hair looks like a flame. It burns so brightly, I swear I can feel the heat.

Standing in the shadows, lurking behind dusty old books, seems undignified. I should make myself known. Test the waters. Maybe she's different. Maybe she can see me. Or even better, hear me.

I imagine, as children, we'd think it would be fun to be invisible. Pretending no one could see us, we'd fantasize we were walking about completely undetected. There's a thrill in not being noticed. Since it's a reality for me, I can say with certainty, it's less glamorous and much more tedious.

But it pales in comparison to never being heard. I can't even begin to describe the deep loneliness I feel having no one to talk to. I'm stuck with my own thoughts, and trust me when I say no one should be burdened with the sole company of themselves for as long as I have. Nothing good can come of it.

A few times, I tried talking to the crabby woman who came by every so often to dust the place. But she never responded. Never looked up from her task at hand. She was always muttering under her breath about someone named Ralph. From the venomous way she said his name, I don't think she likes him very much. I asked her who he was, but again, nothing.

The mystery woman lifts her head, looking as though she were rousing from a deep and satisfying slumber. She rolls her neck and slides her gaze around the room once more. Suddenly, she tenses up, her eyes frozen on some-thing just on her left. Setting her book on the table beside her, she rises out of her seat and stalks in the direction that's caught her attention. Bending down, she retrieves a book off the floor. Without even looking, I know which one it is. *What the Wind Knows* by Amy Harmon. I was flipping through the pages in search of the scene where Thomas first kisses Anne, when the book slipped from my grasp and plummeted to the floor.

Had she heard the sound? Is that what brought her up here?

She whips her head around, and with narrowed eyes,

she scans the baseboards. What is she looking for? A mouse, perhaps?

There aren't any. I could tell her if only she could hear me. There was at one time, though. A little gray wisp of a thing with a long, crooked tail and a broken ear. I called him "Montague or Monty, for short" and for a time, he was my friend. He disappeared one afternoon while I was busy reorganizing the shelves. I never found out what happened to him, but I suspect the grunty woman who hates Ralph may have had something to do with it.

As I watch the woman before me, flicking her eyes from the book in her hands to the room around her, I wonder what she's thinking. I can't be sure, but if I had to guess, I'd say she's trying to come up with a theory for why this book was sitting alone on the floor without anything else around it. There's no table or shelf nearby where it could've fallen from.

On shaky legs, she stands and surveys the room one last time. She squints and shakes her head as though she's trying to talk herself out of a thought. I'd give anything to hear it. There's a part of me—the naive, desperate part—that's sure she's considering *other* alternatives. Alternatives like me.

I don't even know the right word for what I am. A ghost seems strange. I'm not transparent, at least, I don't think I am. I'm not made of mist, and there's no white haze surrounding me. The word spirit makes me sound haunting, and I couldn't be further from that. I'm just a man who spends his days in a hidden library, talking to himself and imagining he is part of the books he reads. Oh, and also, a man who happens to be dead.

This is it. This is my chance. I close my eyes, willing my legs to move, and they do, in microscopic increments, but then I stop. What if she takes one look at me, screams at the top of her lungs, and dashes down the stairs and out of the house forever? That would be … utterly devastating. That sounds so dramatic. I've only just laid eyes on her. But there's something about her. She's much more astute than the snippy older woman. She seems worldly and educated. And absolutely breathtaking. I don't remember any details of my living life, but even if I did, I'm certain no other woman would compare to her. I don't even know her name. Clenching my hands at my sides, I grit my teeth and prepare myself to expect the worst while hoping for the best.

Okay, Jeremy, here goes nothing.

Plunging my hands deep in my pockets to keep them from shaking, I step out into the room. But when I look around, she's gone and so is the book I dropped.

three

DARCY

My body practically vibrates as I float down the stairs. I can't believe there's a hidden library in the house I'm renting. And an incredible one, at that!

Mrs. Fitz said the attic contained items her daughter wasn't able to take with her, but I never expected such an extensive collection of books. When I was looking for a place to live, this town jumped out at me, not only because there was a job vacancy I could fill but also because it called to me in some way. That sounds weird, but I don't know how else to put it. And now that I've uncovered a secret garden, of sorts, I'm even more convinced that I'm exactly where I'm meant to be.

Sinking into the sofa, I turn my attention to the book I'm holding—*What the Wind Knows*. I found it laying in the middle of the floor, which is odd because I can't figure out how it got there. And my mind kept replaying that thud I heard earlier. The one that pulled me up into the attic in the first place. But how could it have fallen, and from where?

My guess is, it wasn't this book I heard. It couldn't have been. I'm still plagued by thoughts of a loose rodent running rampant up there, but I wasn't able to find any noticeable holes.

Who knows how long this book has been sitting on the floor? Maybe Mrs. Fitz's daughter dropped it, or maybe it was this Ralph person. My landlord definitely didn't seem fond of him, and if this collection belongs to her daughter, maybe he didn't see enough value in the books to treat them with care. He couldn't have if he had her jetting off to Hawaii and leaving all of this behind.

I sigh as I run my palm along the cover. This is one of my favorite books, and I think it might be time for a re-read. I know I'm not supposed to be up here, and I'm sure I am *definitely* not supposed to borrow any books, but I'll be careful. Besides, what Mrs. Fitz doesn't know won't hurt her.

My phone rings from my back pocket, startling me out of my reverie. Shit, it's my mom. I never did call her. I was too distracted by the wonderland upstairs.

I swipe the screen, and before I can even press the phone against my ear, she starts. "Darcy? Honey, did you get there safely or are you stuck in a ditch somewhere? Do you need me and Daddy to come rescue you? We can leave right now. And you could come home with us. I know things have been tough around here, but that's small-town life, you know? It'll pass. In fact, I think it already might be. Did I tell you about Grace Tillman? Well, see," she whispers, "according to Peggy—"

"Mom?" The word slices through the air and cuts off her soliloquy. I absolutely hate interrupting people, but with my mom, it's necessary.

"There you are!" She exclaims the words like I was holding back, never mind that she launched into a diatribe without ever pausing to let me speak.

"Here I am," I say with a smile on my face, hoping it comes through in my voice. My mom was not thrilled about my decision to move, and I don't want her to try and talk me into coming back home every time we talk. If she thinks I'm happy, maybe she'll back off.

"Well, it's so good to hear your voice! How was the drive? How's the house? Is it just as nice as it looked in pictures or was it disappointing? It was disappointing, right? Most things are when you only have a picture to go on. You know they say a picture is worth a thousand words, but I've always appreciated reality over pictures. That's when you know something is *for sure*, do you know what I'm saying? It's like—"

I cut in. "The house is amazing, better than amazing, actually. It's like something out of a storybook."

"Oh, you and your stories. I swear, Darcy, you would climb on in to those pages and never look back if you had the chance."

She's not wrong. I've lived hundreds of lives in the pages of books. Most of which I'd trade over my own, even if it were only just for a moment. I rest a hand on the book in my lap. This one most of all.

Glancing at my watch, I'm surprised by the time. How is it already after six? I need to eat and get some rest. I'm meeting with the head librarian, Millicent McGill, tomorrow. Even though it's a Sunday and the library isn't open, she offered to meet with me so I could get a feel for the place before I start work on Monday.

"Hey, Mom, sorry to duck out on you so soon, but I'd

better get a move on. I have some things to take care of before my meeting tomorrow."

"Sure, sure, sure, you go on and take care of yourself. You'll call me tomorrow and let me know how it goes, right?"

"I'll try."

"Darcy Marie Simon, do you think I just tumbled off the apple cart?"

"Of course not," I sigh. "I won't just *try* to call you. I'll actually do it."

"Uh-huh," she says, unconvinced.

She won't relax until I say the words she needs to hear. "I pinky promise."

"Good," she says with a lilt in her voice, and I just know even without seeing her, she has her pinky extended in the air. "Okay, sweetie, go get some rest. We'll talk more tomorrow."

"Bye, Mom. Love you."

"Love you right back," she croons.

I end the call feeling exhausted. My mom means well, but talking to her is sometimes like being hit over the head repeatedly with an empty paper towel roll. It doesn't hurt, but it's annoying as hell, and after a few seconds of it, you're ready to scream.

My stomach erupts in a weighty growl. I haven't had a chance to go grocery shopping yet, but I remember spotting a pizza shop on my way here. It's a quick drive, and within minutes, I'm back at the house, enjoying possibly one of the best slices of pineapple pizza I've ever had. I smirk as I take a bite, remembering how disgusted Chris used to be at my topping preference. It's liberating being able to enjoy it without his constant groaning and mock gagging. Right now, this pizza tastes like freedom, and I savor every bite.

Once I finish eating, I decide to hop in the shower, preparing for an early night. As I'm sudsing my hair, an image flashes in my head. A man. Standing upstairs next to one of the shelves.

My fingers tingle, and my eyes begin frantically bouncing off the walls of the small bathroom. I can't catch my breath as I reach behind me to turn off the water. Grabbing a towel from the bar, I wrap it around myself and twist my wet hair on top of my head.

Was there someone upstairs?

Did I see them, but somehow forgot?

Is that even possible?

I must be imagining it.

After a few seconds of ruminating, I decide that's the only logical explanation. If someone were lurking upstairs, surely, they would've made themselves known. Even if just by accident. It was so quiet; I would've at least heard breathing.

I shake my head. My mom is right. I am forever living in the pages of fiction. And I think that, coupled with exhaustion, has begun to blur the line between reality and imagination.

As I leave the bathroom, I pause in the hallway, eyeing the door to the attic. Hustling into the main bedroom, I grip the wooden chair in front of the vanity. With clumsy hands, I shuffle it out into the hall and shove the end under the doorknob. It probably won't do much good to contain a person if someone were actually up there, which they're not, *but* if I'm wrong and they try to open the door, I'll hear the chair crash on the hardwood floor. Feeling satisfied with my makeshift alarm, I dash back inside the bedroom and close the door, securing the lock. Another precaution I'm grateful for.

Settling under the covers, I stare at the ceiling overhead, chuckling to myself. This has been a whirlwind of a day. It's no wonder I'm imagining things.

Last night I laid down in my childhood bedroom, and twenty-four hours later, I'm over three hundred miles away. It's always fascinated me how far we can travel in such a short amount of time. Both in physical and mental distance. And the perspective that it can give you is immeasurable. I think I already feel better here. It helps that I'm not under the constant watch of judging eyes scrutinizing my every move.

As I close my eyes and drift off to sleep, a vision of a man begins to evolve. In that wistful place between wakefulness and slumber, I catch a glimpse of brown hair shorn close on the sides but longer and fuller on top. His eyes are dark, and his gaze intense as though I'm an intruder, someone he wasn't expecting.

* * *

JEREMY

I've been pacing the room ever since she left, hoping that I haven't missed my chance. I could just make some noise again, but that might scare her away. Then I remember her face as she explored this hidden area. She was mesmerized. And she took my book downstairs with her. Once she's finished with it, she will surely bring it back and choose another. She won't be able to resist the pull. And when she does, I'll be ready.

I need a plan, though. The more I think about it, the

more I'm grateful she wasn't still here when I waltzed into the room. It's been so long since I've been in the company of another person, but it hasn't been long enough for me to be this out of touch. She thinks she's alone in this house, and for the most part, she is. I'm more of a being and less of a human. Stuck somewhere in between. But if the roles were reversed—if I had been in a home thinking I was by myself—and someone just strolled out of hiding, I'd probably defecate in my pants.

It's odd that I'm so certain she'll be able to see and hear me. I'm not sure why I feel so confident. Who's to say she won't be just like the other woman? My head shakes at the thought. Sometimes there are things we just know, and for me, this is one of them.

My eyes flit around the room, landing on the chair she was sitting on. I could wait there. Let her find me the next time she comes up here.

With careful steps, I move toward it, lowering myself onto the cushion. I don't know what's come over me, but I press my nose against the fabric, pulling in a deep inhale. Without working lungs, the feeling is odd. It's as if the air enters my body—or whatever this is—and then dissipates. I can barely remember what it's like to smell something, and I'm not expecting anything, but just as I begin to lift my head, I catch a hint. A faint whiff. A tiny trace. It stirs something inside of me. There's a memory hovering just out of reach, or maybe it's more like a feeling. One word resounds over and over in my head. *Home.* I can't remember where my home was or who I lived with. I don't know any details about my life before I came to be here, and the few memories I do have are just sensory. I can remember what a strawberry tastes like or how it feels to collect snow in my hands and roll it into a ball. But I can't recall people or places.

Her scent lingers for a moment longer, like a clue. But I'm afraid it's part of a mystery I may never solve.

four

DARCY

I awake with a start, snatching my phone off the nightstand. It's a quarter to seven. I was worried I overslept, but my alarm hasn't even had a chance to go off yet.

Kicking the covers off my body, I stretch out on the bed. I had one of those nights where you're aware that you're sleeping. So even though you slept, it isn't restful. I could chalk it up to the new house in a new state with a new job, and sure, that would make anyone anxious, but it's more than that.

My mind drifts to the hidden attic library and those dark eyes I can't seem to stop thinking about. Climbing out of bed, I reach for my robe, sliding it on and cinching it tight at the waist. I'm careful not to make a sound as I unlock the bedroom door, though I don't know why I'm going to such an effort. There's no one else here.

With the door cracked open, I peer out into the hall. My gaze immediately snaps to the attic, where I find the chair I left still shoved underneath the knob. I close my eyes, giving my head a slight shake. "Get a grip, Darcy," I mutter.

The rest of my morning goes by in a blur as I prep for my meeting. Ms. McGill said she'd be at the library from ten to noon, giving me a wide window of time, but I plan to get there right at ten. That way, if she decides she'd like to do something else with her Sunday, she has the option instead of waiting around for me. Plus—and this is the real reason I'm going early—I'm excited to get a feel for the place. I still can't believe how perfect everything seems. This town. This house. The hidden library. I hope my luck continues.

It's only a little after nine, but I think I could probably head out. Even if I'm there early, I could use the time to get more acquainted with the area and plot out the best route to the library from here.

As I pry open the front door, I hear the scratching sound again. It sounds as though it's directly overhead. Glancing at my watch and then up at the stairs, I hover in thought, trying to decide what to do. On a huff, I shove the door closed and trudge up the flight of steps to the second floor.

Tugging the chair away from its spot under the knob, I open the attic door and march up the stairs with purpose. I falter a bit as I near the top. I came up here without a plan. Suppose there *is* a mouse. How am I going to get rid of it?

Hold on a minute. Why is that my problem? If there's a rodent infestation, then it's up to my landlord to take care of it. She'll want to know if I've been snooping around, but I don't have to tell her that part. I can just say I heard the noises from downstairs. That way, I'm not lying. Okay. Now that that's settled, I can quickly check things out and then be on my way.

But as I step into the room, familiar deep-set eyes find mine, holding them captive.

* * *

JEREMY

She can see me! I thought I might be dreaming at first, but no. She's staring at me so intently that I'm not even sure she's breathing. Maybe I should remind her. "Don't forget to breathe, okay? I wouldn't want you to faint." I grin, hoping to encourage a similar reaction from her, but she doesn't look as happy to see me as I am to see her. Or to be seen at all, for that matter.

I continue to speak, hoping to quell the worry she must be feeling. "Sorry. I know how this may seem. Just, um, don't be afraid. I promise I won't hurt you. In fact, I'll stay right over here on this chair and you can stay where you are. Sound good?"

She isn't moving. Have I scared her to death? I better check on her. I start to rise out of my seat, but before I can stand fully, she takes a step back toward the direction she just came from.

"D-don't come any further," she stammers. I can tell she's trying to sound firm, but her voice wavers. She's behaving as though she just came face-to-face with an intruder.

Oh God, she did.

This is not how I wanted things to go. It's only been a few minutes, but already this situation has completely gotten away from me. I'll admit I was impatient sitting for hours waiting. I may have shuffled my feet along the floor, hoping to get her attention. Why did I think that was the right move? She came upstairs and found a stranger sitting in a chair like he belonged up here. Of course, that would terrify her.

I sit back down, holding up my hands. "Don't worry, I won't."

"How?" She scratches at her temple, and I wait for more, but that one word is all she says. I clear my throat, prompting her to continue. It takes her a moment, and then she snaps her fingers. "Wait, you're not Ralph, are you?"

"Christ, I hope not. I never met the guy, but from what I've heard, he's a real bastard."

She squints. "You hope not? What does that mean?"

"Let me rephrase that. I *know* I'm not Ralph. My name is actually Jeremy. Can I ask what your name is?"

"No, you cannot!" She bristles. "How the hell did you get in here, anyway?" Her eyes begin a frantic search of the room with a faraway look like she's trying to uncover a secret hiding place. She finds the spot where I was standing yesterday when she was up here. Pointing, she says, "You were there. I saw you." Her head whips back toward me. "Why didn't you say something? Are you some kind of creep?" She takes another step back. If she's not careful, she's going to fall. I hold out my hand to warn her, but she isn't looking at me. She's shaking her head fervently and speaking in a low whisper. "Of course, he's a creep. He's lurking around in the attic." She looks up at me. "Are you a squatter or something?"

"In a manner of speaking, I suppose I am." I shrug.

She narrows her eyes. "Does Mrs. Fitz know about this?"

"Mrs. Fitz?" I tap my chin, turning the name over in my mind. "Is that the brusque woman who stands about four feet tall?"

She nods cautiously.

"I know *of* her. We've been in each other's company before, but she had no idea."

"So, you've been hiding from her too, huh?" she says, gritting her teeth.

"Not intentionally."

"You're talking in riddles, and I've been standing here, allowing it to continue for way too long. Whatever this shit is, it's done now." She spins on her heel and starts to leave.

"Wait!" I call out, rising to my feet. "You haven't let me explain."

"Oh, I've let you say enough, considering you're trespassing. You can save your *story* for the police," she calls over her shoulder.

I move in her direction, tentative at first, but I quicken my steps when it's obvious she's made up her mind. "Please, you don't understand."

"I think I do." She lunges toward the little wooden table on her right and grabs an oversized copy of *Gone with the Wind*. Without hesitation, she whirls around, hurling the book at me. Her aim is impeccable as it sails through the air and plunges into my chest. But it doesn't stop there. It continues moving, passing through my body and landing with a *thud* on the floor behind me.

We both stare at it, and then I turn to face her, finding her eyes still glued to the book. "I never liked that book. If you ask me, it shouldn't be revered as a classic. The floor is a fitting place for it." I chuckle, but she doesn't seem interested in my opinion.

Her jaw is slack, and her eyes are wide. "What the fuck?" She wobbles on her feet. Her breaths come out in short puffs.

"So, here's the thing," I say slowly. "I'm not actually alive anymore."

"Shut up," she snaps.

"But I—"

"Just shut up. I can't hear this." She presses her palms into her eyes, rubbing frantically. "No. Uh-uh. This isn't happening. I'm just tired. It was a long day of travel yesterday and then I didn't sleep well and it's just all catching up to me. Yep, that's it. It's gotta be. Okay, I'm gonna go. And when I come back, you won't be here because you never actually were, right? Right."

I cock my head, studying her, unsure if I should interrupt. She seems to be having a full conversation with herself. Problem is, she's wrong. This is definitely happening. I'm dead, and I'm also standing right in front of her. But I have no experience with this. She's the first person to ever actually see me.

She looks up, searching my face for a moment, and the oddest sensation comes over me. It's similar to how I felt when I smelled her on the chair last night. Then she closes her eyes and shakes her head rapidly.

The chunky soles of her shoes clomp on the wooden steps as she quickly descends. The door closes with a soft click, and I hear the muted sound of something being pressed up against it. Interesting. If she's so convinced I'm not real, then why is she trying to keep me trapped up here?

It's only when she's gone that I realize I never did learn her name. It's okay. I can wait. She'll be back, and when she is, she'll have no choice but to let me explain.

five

DARCY

I run down the stairs and right out the front door, never once looking back. I don't know what's happening to me, but I'm convinced it's nothing that some fresh air and a brand-new library can't fix. And then when I come home, whatever that was in the attic will be over. It sounds so convincing in my head, so why don't I believe it?

Enough of that. I wasted too much time already. It's ten thirty. I wanted to be at the library a half hour ago.

Dashing to my car, I try to keep my movements more in line with someone running a few minutes late and less like a person running from their haunted house. I'm not sure how successful I am, but I didn't notice anyone outside, so maybe no one saw me.

I twist the knob on the stereo and zone out on music as I drive to the library. But even as I try to suppress intrusive thoughts, I keep coming back to the way that book passed right through him. Did I imagine that? And what did he say his name was? Jeremy?

Nope. He *didn't* say his name because *he* isn't real.

"The Night We Met" by Lord Huron comes on the radio, and I crank the volume, drowning out visions I'm not equipped to handle. I can't let my thoughts drift to dangerous places. I'm meeting with my new boss in a few minutes. It's important to keep my composure. She hired me as a children's librarian. First impressions are vital, especially when you'll be working with kids.

The library sits on a quiet, tree-lined street. Another picture-perfect setting. This town keeps showing up for me. And if not for what just transpired at the house, I'd still be walking on air at the idea that I get to live here. But now, there's a tiny fracture in that happy little bubble. A microscopic fissure, but still a crack, nonetheless.

I flip my visor down and check my reflection. My cheeks are slightly flushed, but otherwise, there's no sign of internal turmoil.

I give myself a pep talk. "Okay, books have always been your life. That's not going to change, but maybe Mom's right. The stories are starting to get to you and your imagination is in overdrive. But you've got this. This job is a dream, and this is where you're supposed to be." I nod several times, drilling the words into my brain. I felt like I belonged the moment I entered this town. There's a familiarity here—one I can so easily lean into. I'm not about to let some crazy one-off hallucination mess it up for me.

I exit the car feeling more confident and determined than I did entering it. Pulling my shoulders back and lifting my chin, I stride to the glass double doors with purpose.

A slight woman wearing black leggings and an oversized worn hoodie is crouched on the floor by the new release shelf. A bevy of books fans out around her as she plucks them one by one off the ground, sliding them onto the shelves. Her casual outfit has me second-guessing my decision to wear boots and a fitted knee-length skirt.

She cranes her neck to glance back at the door and finds me standing there. I give her a quick wave, and she smiles. Dusting her hands off on her pants, she stands, extending an arm to me. "You must be Darcy. It's wonderful to finally meet you."

I amble toward her, grasping her hand in my own. "Hi, Ms. McGill. It's so nice to meet you as well."

She lets go of my hand, flapping hers. "Oh, please, call me Milly. We're anything but formal around here. Now," she says, clucking her tongue, "let's get you situated."

Milly leads me through the front room, giving me a quick tour. She waves her arms wildly, gesticulating in all directions. She stops short, clasping her hands at her chest. "Listen to me go on and on. Your head is probably spinning. Don't worry," she says, patting my arm. "You'll get the hang of the place soon enough."

I smile at her, deciding not to remind her that the library I worked at before this one was located in a large city. The nonfiction section alone eclipsed this entire building. "I'm sure I will," I say. "Everything is so well organized. I can't tell you how much I appreciate that."

"Well," she hums, tucking a slip of gray hair behind her ear. "That's sure nice to hear."

People always assume that librarians are meticulous and orderly, and when it comes to the books in our care, that's usually true, but most of us are here because we have a deep love of literature. Our passion is so extreme it preoccupies our thoughts, making for a very cluttered person. The library I interned at in college was the very embodiment of living in a haze of written words. There were stacks of books precariously clustered on the floor in disorganized piles. Loose papers and discarded check-out cards littered the place as though they were a new type of carpet. George, the man who oversaw the library, spent most of his time nestled in a comfortable recliner, his nose pressed among the pages of the newest fantasy novel. He cared more for the words on the page than for the books themselves. Even though I could empathize, it made it clear there were better ways to conduct a library. And just from this short walk through, I can already tell Milly has the right idea.

"Over here," she says, pointing to a quaint little corner on the right, "is our children's section. It isn't much, but I'm hoping you can change all of that." She beams at me.

My eyes surf the space, picking up tiny details along the way. An adorable hand-painted scene from *The Very Hungry Caterpillar* adorns the wall and in front of it sits a large plush area rug shaped like a leaf. It's the perfect spot for weekly story time. "It looks pretty spectacular to me," I say with a breathy voice.

She grins. "It's come a long way, that's for sure. But I am certain you can take it even further. We may not have the biggest library, but we make up for it with our generous patrons. There's a very nice budget set aside for this area." With a clap of her hands, she proclaims, "Okay! I'll leave you to it. Come and find me if you have any questions. And Darcy?"

"Yes?"

"I'm really glad you're here." She scurries off to continue filling shelves, leaving me standing there, once again, feeling lucky.

I spend the next hour acquainting myself with the setup. The more time I spend, the more I realize what Milly was hinting at. The area is adorable, but it's also kind of generic. I think we could do a lot more to make it stand out and be more inviting to kids. If we want to encourage young readers, we have to appeal to what they love. And what they love is creative play.

The morning passes by quickly, and by the time I'm ready to leave, I have a long list of ideas that I share with Milly.

"This is amazing, Darcy!" she exclaims. "See, this is exactly what I was talking about. All righty, why don't you leave this list with me and I'll have a talk with the board about releasing some funds. Sound good?"

"Sounds perfect." I nod.

I leave the library feeling much lighter. This is exactly the change in scenery I needed. After my "scandal," my hometown became a place I didn't recognize anymore. It didn't take me long to realize there was nothing for me there. For the first time since leaving, I feel proud of myself.

Sucking in a big breath, I look around at the beautiful grounds surrounding the library. "This is gonna be good," I say, letting the air rush back out.

* * *

JEREMY

The front door creaks as it opens. I have no idea how long she was gone. In some ways, it feels like an eternity, and in others, only a matter of minutes. When you're dead, time is subjective. Most days go by with me barely registering it's happened. The only indication is the changing light outside.

Nervous energy courses through my nonexistent body. I'm not proud of it, but I lie down on the ground, pressing my ear against the floor. I can make out a bit of movement, but not enough. Right now, time is still. Suspended.

I assumed when she came home, she'd come barreling up here, determined to prove the events of earlier never happened. So I'm surprised when she doesn't seem to be in any hurry. A distressing thought pops into my head. What if she's decided to never come back up here? Yesterday, I heard her say something about not being able to stay away, but has she changed her mind? God, I hope not.

I've been alone in this room for so long with an endless supply of books to keep me company. But now that I finally have someone to talk to, I can't handle the thought of losing her. I'll give her some time, but if she doesn't come back, I'll make it impossible for her to ignore me.

I'm still lying on the floor when I hear her padding up the stairs to the second floor. Tiny thumps sound as she moves toward the attic door. There's a pause, and then the thumping starts again, moving away from the door. It goes on like this, back and forth, for a while until I hear the soft scrape of her removing whatever it was she placed in front of the door. And then it opens.

She's moving so quickly, there isn't time for me to get up from where I'm lying. I try to push myself up to sitting, but she's in the room before I have a chance. She scans the book-lined walls like she's putting off the inevitable. She hasn't glanced my way, but she must know I'm here. And then it happens.

Her eyes find mine. "God damn it," she curses.

I sit up. "You know, that may be the case, actually. After all, if there is a heaven, it's clear I'm not welcome up there. But if being eternally damned means I get to spend my time here with every book I could ever wish for, maybe it's not so bad." I shrug, giving her a crooked smile.

"So, it's true then?" She grips her waist with her hand like she's trying to keep herself upright. I notice she hasn't ventured all the way into the room, preferring to stay close to the exit.

"That I'm a ghost, you mean?"

She nods, reluctantly.

"Yes, that is true." I tip my head, regarding her with curiosity, eager to see how she handles this information.

She scrubs a hand over her face and casts her eyes to the ceiling, peering out of the skylight overhead. She stays that way, immobile, lost in thought, for a few seconds or maybe minutes. I can't be sure the length of time, although, from where I'm still sitting on the floor, it feels too long. She might be in shock.

I rise to my feet, and her head whips in my direction. Her eyes widen and then narrow as they scrutinize me.

"You don't look like a ghost."

I cock my head. "So, you've spent some time in the company of dead people then?"

"Huh?" Her face pinches.

"Well, if I don't look like a ghost, I'm guessing you must have some experience with them."

She rolls her eyes. "No, I just mean that, uh, well, you know."

"I'm afraid I don't," I say, shaking my head.

"Are you always this difficult?" She huffs.

"Difficult?" I lay a hand on my chest, affronted. "I'm just trying to figure you out, is all."

"Well, that makes two of us."

six

DARCY

He's staring at me. It's unnerving but also intriguing. And I hate that. None of this should be intriguing. None of this should be happening.

"Listen," he says. "You're looking a little pale. Why don't you come have a seat?" He gestures at the wingback chair to his right.

I'm looking pale? Is he for real? No, I guess he isn't. I suppress an ill-timed chuckle, but he still seems to clock it. His mouth curves with amusement. Wait. He can't read minds, can he?

"Do you know what I'm thinking?" I ask, hating the waver in my voice.

"What are you thinking?" He seems confused.

"Nothing. Forget I asked."

His eyes widen slightly, but he doesn't press me further. Instead, he waves a hand toward the chair. He's very persistent.

I do as he says and amble toward the chair on shaky legs. I'm not sure why I'm taking orders from a ghost, except I do feel a little weak at the moment. Sitting seems like a good idea. I plop onto the cushion with an ungraceful moan. His brow lifts, but he says nothing. He backs away and leans against a table. I appreciate the gesture.

Crossing his arms over his chest, he says, "Now, let's start over, shall we? You said I didn't look like a ghost. Is that because I'm not wearing a white sheet with holes cut out for my eyes?" He smirks.

"Yeah, smart-ass, that's exactly it." I groan. "Also, you forgot to glow."

"Glow?"

"Uh-huh, didn't you watch any TV as a kid? You should be transparent, but you're not. And you should have like a halo or a haze around you. Something to help you appear less human and more, you know, dead." I gulp as I say the word. I can't believe I'm having this conversation.

"Huh. I guess I must've missed the memo," he offers.

"I guess so." I nod, and so does he, and then we just stare at each other. Neither one of us speaks for some time. It should be awkward or even terrifying, at least for me—after all, he's a ghost—but it's neither. It's oddly comforting.

"You know," he muses, "for someone who's just seen a ghost, you seem pretty relaxed."

Okay, that's the second time he's done that. "You can read my mind, can't you?"

His posture wilts. "I'm sorry?"

"You know what I'm thinking. You're in my head right now, aren't you? I'll prove it. Tell me what number I'm thinking of." I lean forward in my seat with my hands on my knees, a challenging gleam in my eye. I repeat the number four over and over inside my mind, daring him to prove me wrong.

"Hmm." He taps his chin. "Let's see. Oh! It's nine hundred and ninety-seven, right?"

"Not even close." I scoff, sitting up and pressing my back into the seat. "How do I know you're not lying?"

"You don't." He shrugs. "But if I were, then I wouldn't have so many questions for you. I'd already know the answers."

"Questions? What kind of questions?"

"Well, for starters," he quips. "What's your name?"

"It's Darcy." As soon as I say my name, the strangest thing happens. His entire face seems to light up, and his lips begin to move. I wait for a sound, but it doesn't come. It takes me a moment to realize he's mouthing my name over and over like he's tasting it.

"It's very nice to meet you, Darcy." His words are loaded with so much sincerity it stuns me. "I don't know if you remember from earlier or if you even heard me, but allow me to officially introduce myself. I'm Jeremy."

I nod. I remember, despite trying desperately to forget. "How long have you been up here?" I expect a simple answer—something along the lines of four years. Instead, Jeremy offers a response that only brings more questions.

"I don't know."

I must've heard wrong. "You don't know?"

He shakes his head.

"Well, when did you die? How did you die? You must know something about how you came to be here."

He looks away, forlorn. And then he whispers those same words again, "I don't know."

* * *

JEREMY

Any minute now, she's going to bolt. I'm sure of it. I didn't expect her to ask the hard-hitting questions so fast, but why wouldn't she? She just found a ghost in her attic. Of course, she's going to want to know how I got here and why.

I'm about to offer more of an explanation when she starts to stammer. "Shit. That was rude, wasn't it? I'm sorry. I usually have a lot more tact, but this is not an area I have much experience in. I don't have *any* experience in it, actually. But now that I think about it, asking a ghost how they died is probably right up there with asking a woman when her baby is due before she confirms she's even pregnant. I just—"

"It's okay. I don't think there's a guidebook for this sort of thing, you know?"

"Are you sure? Have you looked up here? Maybe there's a *Handbook for the Recently Deceased* lying around somewhere." She chuckles, and I get the feeling she's made a clever joke, but it's one I don't understand. When she notices my confusion, she adds, "Okay, so judging by the look on your face, I'd say you've been dead for quite a while. At least, before 1988."

"That's an oddly specific year."

She laughs, and it's the best sound I think I've ever heard. "Yeah, what I said before about a handbook, it was a movie reference."

"Aha." I nod, smiling. "So, tell me, Darcy. Here you are sitting across from a dead guy and yet you're making jokes and talking about movies. I can't be sure, but I'd guess most people would've run out of here screaming the moment they saw me."

She shrugs. "You're not particularly frightening unless ..."

I uncross my arms and grasp the table behind me. "Unless what?"

"You aren't planning to," her throat bobs with a hard swallow, "you know, possess my body, are you?"

"Hmm." I scratch my jaw. "That thought hadn't occurred to me, but now that you bring it up." I take a step toward her. She responds immediately, pulling back and tucking her legs underneath her. She covers her face with shaky hands. "Whoa, I was joking," I say, though she doesn't look up. Great. Now I've really gone and done it.

I take a few tentative steps her way and reach out my hand. It's so close to touching hers, yet I know if I do, neither one of us will feel a thing. This is the first true conversation I've had, and I'm not ready for the jolt of reality to hit when I reconfirm the inevitable. I'm dead and she's not. I let my arm fall, and my hand smacks against my leg. She looks up, finding me much closer to her than I was when she first closed her eyes. "It's okay," I say, holding up my hands and backing away. "I'm not going to hurt you, though I don't know how to make you believe that. And I honestly can't blame you if you never do."

She slowly uncurls herself. "I believe you," she whispers.

"You do?" I'm astounded.

"I do," she says, her head nodding. "I can't say why that is. I haven't got a clue except, well, I'm a gullible idiot." She half shrugs, and her lips curve into a small smile.

I smile back. "That must be it. And while we're being honest, I suppose I should tell you that before you came up here, I was lying on the floor trying to hear you. Looks like I'm an idiot, too."

A laugh bursts out of her, surprising us both. "I should probably be horrified by that, but the idea of you on the floor with your ear pressed against the ground is just too funny." I join her, laughing at my stupidity.

Our laughter dies off slowly, dissipating into the air with a few final haha's. And I know I should take us back to her earlier questions. "You asked me how I died and how long I've been up here." She starts to protest, but I hold up my hand, stopping her. "It's okay. Those are fair questions and I'm aware of how weird it is that I can't answer them. I've just been up here and it's been long enough to see the gruff woman a few times when she popped in to dust and rearrange a few things. I tried to talk to her, but she never heard or saw me. I just assumed after that I'd be alone. I knew I was dead, but that was about it. Then you came along and those rules I thought were set in stone don't seem to apply to you."

She tilts her head, studying me as though I'm a curious code she's trying to decipher. A slow smile spreads on her face. "Maybe it *is* true."

I give her a lopsided grin. "What's that?"

"Well, it's another movie reference—actually the same one as before. Basically, the only people who can see the dead are strange and unusual. I guess I made the cut." She chuckles.

"You don't seem all that strange to me."

"You'd be surprised," she says, tugging at her lip.

Now I'm intrigued. I want to ask her for more detail, but she stands up, effectively cutting my thoughts off at the quick.

"Well, Jeremy, this has been ... interesting." She quirks a

brow. "But I should really get some things done before my day is over."

"Of course. I don't want to keep you," I lie. I'd keep her up here with me for hours if I could. It's nice to have the company.

She strolls toward the stairs, stopping just before she reaches them. Turning to look over her shoulder, she stuns me with arresting eyes. Light filters in through the skylight just above her, bathing her face in a glow that's intensified by the green in her eyes. "Can I, um, bring you anything?"

"I don't eat or drink anything, you know, since I'm dead." I mean it as a joke, but she grimaces, and I immediately wish I could take the words back. "Listen, being up here surrounded by books isn't much of a hardship. I'll be fine." I punctuate it with a smile and it seems to ease her previous discomfort.

"Okay, I'm just downstairs if you change your mind."

I give her a small wave, and she saunters down the stairs. The door closes softly, and a few seconds later, I hear the sound of her sliding something against the knob. It surprises me, though maybe it shouldn't. I thought we had a connection or at least graduated to acquaintances. But maybe that isn't possible, or maybe I just have my work cut out for me.

seven

DARCY

I flop backward onto my bed, trying to catch my breath.

There's a ghost in my attic. A specter. A spirit. A phantom. All words I've read about but never believed to be true. But there's no denying it now. He looks so real, but a literal book flew right through his chest like he was nothing more than a shadow.

And he doesn't know how he died or why he's in this house. That's even more bizarre. I have so many questions. But I don't think he'll have the answers.

Scrubbing a hand over my face, I'm shocked by how calm I remained up there. I was ready to run screaming out of the house when I thought a mouse might be roaming around, but once I found out it was a ghost, I sat down and had a little chat with him. The thing is, being in his presence didn't feel odd. In fact, it felt natural, almost as if I'd done it before. I blow out a breath. This is a lot to absorb.

I wonder if he's somehow connected to this house. He

must be if he materialized here. Grabbing my phone off my nightstand, I do a quick search online, typing the address into the search bar. Nothing of note comes up in the results besides a Google map and a few hits on some real estate sites, including the listing that I originally answered. Maybe the library has some sort of digital archive I can search. I'll check next time I'm there. If I can figure out how he came to be here, maybe I can help him move on somehow.

Despite our relaxed conversation, I still shoved the chair under the doorknob again, even though I felt kind of foolish. I mean, he's a ghost. Can't he just pass right through the door?

Hold on. If he can move through objects, then how can I be sure he won't come in here at night while I'm sleeping.

I sit up, raking my fingers through my hair. My entire body erupts in goose bumps. Can he do that?

I leap from the bed and begin frantically dashing through the house like I'm looking for something. But for what, I have no idea. Maybe my common sense will pop up somewhere since I seem to have lost it along the way.

I'm back in the hallway facing the attic door when I hear Jeremy's voice calling from above.

"Darcy? You don't have to worry about me coming down there. I can't leave this room."

"You can't?" My voice is barely above a whisper, but he hears me anyway.

"Nope. So, you can stop fretting and relax. I mean, as much as you can with a ghost living in your attic." He laughs. Of course, he laughs. He's so blasé about all of this. I don't know how he remains so calm, considering he's dead. And now, knowing he's trapped in the attic. I can't say I'd be all that relaxed about it if I were him.

"How'd you know I was worried?" I ask the question against my better judgment. I've just admitted to being afraid of him, and I don't know why, but that makes me feel guilty. Like I should know better.

"Are you kidding?" he asks. "Your thoughts are so loud, I can't concentrate. I've read the same sentence four times already."

My body tenses and my fingers feel numb. He said he couldn't hear my thoughts.

"It's a joke, Darcy," he tsks. "The truth is, I heard you running around the house and thought you might be getting ready to leave. I wouldn't blame you if you had, but it's been really nice being seen and heard. I'm not ready for it to end."

My heart sinks. Is this how death is? Completely void of contact and trapped in a makeshift prison? I feel the sudden need to reassure him. "I may have been freaking out."

"I knew it!"

"Hold on. Let me finish," I scold.

"Sorry, go on."

I smile. This is so weird, and yet, talking to him this way —without seeing him—is easier. Less intimidating. It feels almost like chatting with a friend. "This house is too good to be true. I mean, the neighborhood is nice; it's conveniently located, and don't even get me started on the crazy low rent. And the secret attic library is an incredible discovery, even if I do have to share it with a dead guy." He chuckles. It's deep and low and soothing in a way I can't explain. "So, yeah, I think we can make this work."

"Good." I can hear the smile in his voice.

There are so many things I should be doing, but right now, all I want to do is keep talking to him. "What are you reading, anyway?"

He clears his throat. "Um, it's nothing you've probably heard of."

I doubt that. I'm a librarian. Books are my thing. "Try me." I smirk, hoping he can hear it in my voice.

There's a pause before he answers, and it's long enough to make me wonder if he's planning on leaving me hanging. "It's just a story about a young girl who goes to live with her dad and meets some new and interesting people who are very different than she is."

"Huh, that does sound intriguing." And also, vaguely like a series of books I read several years ago, but he can't be talking about those. Can he? "What's the name?"

"What's that?" he stammers.

"The name of the book. What is it?"

"Uh, I'm not sure."

"You're not sure?" I cock my head at the ceiling. Now I'm intrigued. "There isn't a title anywhere on it? Have you checked the cover?"

"Fine," he huffs. "I'm reading *Twilight*."

Even though he can't see me, I press the back of my hand to my mouth, concealing my lips as they curve into a huge smile.

"Come on. Don't laugh," he groans.

"I'm not laughing. I'm just surprised, is all."

"Why? Because you think I should be reading Hemingway or something."

"Oh God, no. No one should be reading that."

"Color me curious, Miss Darcy. Do tell. What do you have against Hemingway?" His voice carries an air of amusement. We can't see each other, but I picture him sitting on the floor. His legs are splayed out in front of him, and his back is pressed against the chair. He feels close to me somehow, even though he's on a different floor of the house. Neither one of us has to raise our voices, yet we can hear each other clearly. It's kind of like talking on the phone, but more intimate. I don't hate it, but for now, I'm going to ignore how that revelation makes me feel.

"Please." I scoff. "It would take me less time to list anything I have *for* that vile man. He belongs nowhere near the cannon."

"I won't argue there."

My eyes widen. "You won't?" I don't know much about Jeremy, but he strikes me as an academic. I can usually spot one a mile away since I'm one myself. Most of us love Hemingway, but not me. I stuck out like a sore thumb in grad school.

"No. He sucks."

I laugh and it's the kind that comes out in wheezes that are barely audible. Tears instantly spring from my eyes and I double over.

"Wow, I've never thought of myself as a comedian before, but perhaps I should reconsider. I'm sure a true master of comedy would never ask such a question, but what exactly did I say that was so funny?"

It takes me a moment to catch my breath, and when I do, I have to choke back more laughter threatening to burst from my mouth like a geyser. "See! That right there. The way you talk. It's like you're from another time. And then you go and say something simple and modern like 'he sucks.' I don't know you very well, but it seemed out of character for you and really freaking hilarious." I chuckle.

"Ahh, well, maybe Bella and her vampires are influencing me."

"Ha, ha, yeah, maybe that's it." I tug at my lip, fluttering my lashes at the ceiling. Oh shit, am I flirting with a ghost? Jesus, Darcy, get a hold of yourself. I blink several times and shake my head. No, of course, I'm not. After the situation I left back home, this conversation is just a refreshing change of pace. Nothing more to it.

* * *

JEREMY

I want to hear her laugh again. Being up here for as long as I have, I'd forgotten how impactful basic human connection is. And making her laugh, well, it's up there at the top of my greatest accomplishments. Since I have no lasting memories, it's not a long list—composed mostly of having read the complete works of Shakespeare and Homer's *The Iliad and The Odyssey*. But now I can place "making Darcy laugh" at the very top. It brings a strange sense of contentment.

Speaking of Darcy, she's been quiet for a while. Maybe she's no longer there. Earlier, she said she had things to do, and I can't expect her to just stand there and entertain me.

"Are you there?" Her voice has a slight lilt. Is it hopefulness I'm hearing?

I respond quickly. "I am. Of course, it's not like I have much choice." I chuckle, hoping she'll join me. She doesn't. And when she speaks again, her tone is more melancholy.

"That's true. For what it's worth, I'm sorry about that."

"Don't be. I'm not." It's the first time I've said those words and meant them. At this moment, I feel like the luckiest ghost in the stratosphere.

"How can you say that? Don't you feel trapped?"

"Well, I can't leave, so I suppose trapped is one way to describe it. But I also can't *feel* anything. I just exist wherever I am and right now, that's in a magical hidden library in the middle of small-town suburbia."

She hums, sounding as though she's lost in thought. "How do you know you're in a small town?"

"Darcy." I scoff. "Give me a little credit. I can see quite a bit from these windows and I've read about enough small towns to know what to look for."

"Is that so?" she asks in a challenging tone.

"Mm-hmm. The signs are everywhere. White picket fences, tiny window boxes filled with flowers, little garden gnomes peeking out behind carefully manicured shrubbery, a swing set in every yard. I could go on and on. But, please, tell me I'm wrong. I don't like to be wrong, but if I am, I'll admit defeat."

She laughs, but it's more of a giggle, and I like it a lot. More than I should. "You're right, but you're also ridiculous."

"No one's disputing that." The grin on my face is so wide that I think it might hurt if I could feel my face.

A few seconds pass, and then I hear a quiet gasp. "Wow, okay, it's somehow after seven and I haven't eaten dinner or done any of my prep work for tomorrow."

I should let her go; tell her we can talk more tomorrow, but I just need a few more minutes with her. "What's so special about tomorrow?"

"It's my first day at my new job." Her voice vibrates with excitement.

"And where's that?"

"Well, it just so happens, you are speaking to the new children's librarian at Baker Hill Library."

I barely know her, but I am certain there is no other job on earth more suited for her. "Impressive! They're lucky to have you."

"I'm the lucky one. Anyway, I'll talk to you soon since, you know, you're kind of shacking up in my attic," she says in a humorous tone.

"I am, indeed. If you need me, you know where to find me."

"Good night, Jeremy."

I close my eyes, holding on to the way she says my name. It's an otherwise ordinary name. I don't know where it came from or why I'm so sure it's mine. But hearing it come out of her mouth, it sounds as if it were meant for a duke or a king, someone much more important than me. "Good night, Darcy."

I've been lying on the floor since I first heard her sprinting around the house earlier. Now, as we say our good nights, I roll onto my side, pressing my ear firmly to the wooden floor. I can't hear a sound and am just about to sit up when the faint creak of a floorboard catches my ear. It's followed by another and another. I track her movements to somewhere on my left, and then they disappear. It's as if she's stumbled into an abyss.

Or maybe it's me. After all, I'm the one out here, lost in some undetermined realm that blurs the line between the living and the dead. Only right now, I don't think I'm lost. And for a guy who doesn't feel things, this sure seems a lot like happiness.

eight

DARCY

"There you are!" Milly exclaims, causing me to jolt and fumble the coffee mug in my hands. Thankfully, I manage to grab a hold of it before it falls. Sliding it onto the counter in the break room, I say a silent prayer of thanks that I hadn't yet had a chance to fill it with coffee.

Milly's eyes are the size of silver dollars. "Nice save!"

"Thanks," I say with a grimace.

"I'm sorry I startled you. I thought you saw me walk in, but I was wrong. Still dealing with some residual first day jitters?" She winks and gives me a warm smile. It soothes the harsh edge of embarrassment I was feeling.

"I guess I am." I chuckle, although it's not nervous energy that makes me jump. I was daydreaming. Lost in thoughts of a certain attic-dwelling ghost. I thought I'd hear from him this morning once he heard me awake and moving around in the house. I wasn't quiet on purpose, hoping for one of his little barbs, some smart-ass quip fired down at me from his perch above. But nothing ever came, and I've been doing my best to block out the haze of disappointment ever since. It's managed to sneak up on me the few times I've found myself alone today. I've tried to consider why he chose to stay silent. He's a ghost, so it wasn't like he was sleeping, and he can't leave the attic, so it certainly wasn't because he'd gone out. Maybe he thought I needed to focus on what I was doing, and he didn't want to distract me. Or maybe he was lost in a book. I've been there myself—many times—so I can definitely see how that could happen. Whatever it was, he had his reasons. I'm sure when I get home, he'll be more than ready to chat.

"So, listen," Milly leans in, dropping her voice to just above a whisper, "Paige and her dad, Silas, are here." She arcs her brow but doesn't elaborate.

"O-o-kay," I say, enunciating every letter. "And, is Silas on the board or something?" There's obviously a reason why these people are important. I'm not sure why she's being so cagey about it.

"No, no, it's nothing like that. It's just more that … well, come have a look for yourself." She grins in an odd way like she's in on a joke that's clearly over my head. Then she saunters out of the room, leaving me hanging.

If there's one thing I can't stand, it's theatrics. I had enough of that from the thespians in college. I roll my eyes and turn back to my abandoned mug. Filling it with equal parts coffee and sugar, I top it off with a generous helping of half-and-half. With my cup in hand, I straighten my back and stride out into the library.

Letting my eyes roam around the room, I don't see anyone besides Cliff. He's a retired English teacher who I've quickly learned enjoys spending the bulk of his days hiding out here in order to avoid the expansive "honey do list" his wife created for him. He gives me a salute, and I nod, smiling. I have no idea who this Paige and her dad, Silas, are, but maybe they'll come into my section while they're here and I can introduce myself to them then. From the way Milly talked about them, I can only imagine they must be noteworthy.

I turn to my right, and my elbow jabs something hard, causing the mug in my hand to jostle and spray lukewarm coffee all over the front of my favorite white sweater. "Ah! Son of a—" Crystal blue eyes peer up at me, stopping me in my tracks. They belong to a tiny human with long blond hair. She's gripping the leg of someone and attempting to hide behind it. "Billy goat!" I add, albeit unconvincingly.

Stepping back, I swipe my hand over the moisture on my sweater while finding my kindest smile for the traumatized little girl. "Hello there! What's your name?"

"It's Paige." The voice that responds is deep and gravelly and most certainly does not belong to the child cowering before me. I lift my head to find those same clear blue eyes, only these reside in a much older face. A face that's inherently masculine, with a strong chin and chiseled cheekbones. It's the kind of face that seems nearly perfect with no noticeable defects. It's also not unpleasant to look at. The lips are thin, but when they smile, they seem fuller. It's only when they let out a gruff chuckle that I realize I'm staring.

I avert my gaze, but it's too late. It must've looked like I was ogling him. Great. This is obviously the guy Milly was telling me about, and what a great first impression I've made. First, I douse myself in coffee, then I nearly swear in front of his child, and as if that wasn't enough, I openly gawk at him. I wish I could just dart away, but that would only make things more awkward. So, I reach down into the depths of myself and pull out whatever minuscule scraps of self-confidence remain. What I find isn't much, but I can work with it. I lift my chin and look up at him. "Hi, you must be Silas. I'm Darcy, the new children's librarian. Milly's told me so much about you, the both of you," I lie. She hasn't said much aside from urging me to look. And standing here in front of Mr. tall, dark, and dreamy, I can understand why.

"She has, huh?" His mouth quirks. Is he trying not to laugh?

"Sorry about earlier," I say sheepishly.

He chuckles. "Why are you apologizing? I walked into your elbow. I should be the one saying sorry."

"It's no biggie." I shrug.

"You sure? I mean, your sweater tells a different story." His eyes flick down and then immediately back up. Something changes in his eyes. There's a fire behind them that wasn't there before.

"I should probably go deal with that, but I hope we get to catch up before you leave. Paige," I say, looking down at the timid little girl, "I just got a brand-new set of colored markers and I could use your help to make sure they all work. Think you're up for the job?"

She looks up at her dad and then back at me, her eyes wide and earnest. "Uh-huh!"

"Great! Let me run to the bathroom and then I'll meet you over in the children's section, deal?"

"Deal," she says, giving me a small but beautiful smile.

I catch Silas's eyes for a brief moment before rushing off in search of the bathroom. He looks amused, and I'm not sure how I feel about that.

Once I'm inside the bathroom, I lean against the door,

feeling my face flush. I need to get a grip. So, he's a decent-looking guy—more than decent, but that's beside the point. He's a dad, and even though I didn't look for a wedding ring, I'm pretty sure I'd find one if I did.

Setting my mug in the sink, I turn on the faucet, letting the water warm up. I glance up, catching sight of myself in the mirror. "Holy shit!" I exclaim in horror as I survey the damage. The coffee spill is smack dab over my chest and has not only soaked through my sweater but also my bra. The wet fabric sticks to my skin like a scuba suit, and with my nipples standing at attention, it leaves little to the imagination.

I smack my palm to my forehead. I cannot believe this is happening. Fortunately, I keep an extra set of clothes in my trunk. Working with kids in the past, you learn quickly, and it's not the first time I've needed a wardrobe change. Unfortunately, I need to leave this room to go get it.

What are the chances I can manage doing all of that without Silas spotting me? Given everything that's happened up to this point, I'd say it's somewhere between zero and nada.

* * *

JEREMY

By the way the light changes outside, I can tell the day is passing. If I had a clock in here and any idea of Darcy's work schedule, I'd be able to better determine when she might be home, but for now, I just have to hope it's soon.

I wanted to say something this morning when I heard her rushing around beneath me, but I didn't want to bother

her or, worse—come across as needy. I cringe. Still, I had thought she might call up to me, even if just to say goodbye.

And then, when I finally decided to wish her well, it was too late. I called out, "Good luck on your first day!" just as she closed the door. I've been chastising myself ever since.

These feelings are foreign. What a strange turn of events this is. I've grown used to just existing up here. My only friends were fictional characters. Now here I am fretting over not saying good morning to a woman I only just met.

But she isn't *just* a woman that I met. She's the only person I've encountered who can see and hear me. And to be acknowledged after living in the shadows for so long is indescribable.

I need to be careful. I don't want to scare her off, but I also need to be prepared for her to leave on her own someday. She's renting this place now, but I can't expect her to stay here forever. And right now, I feel as though I'm on the precipice of something that has the potential to destroy me, but it also might be exactly what I need to move on. I can't put my finger on it. It's only just a feeling at this point, but Darcy is important in a way I've yet to determine. Her renting this place wasn't an accident. It feels like she's here for me, or maybe I'm here for her.

The front door closes with a tinny click, causing me to sit up straight. Running a hand through my hair, I find myself wishing I had a mirror, which is absurd because even if I did, I doubt I'd be able to see myself in it.

Darcy's footsteps move around the first floor with purpose. It's harder to hear her when she's down there, but I think she may be humming. That seems like a sign she had a good day.

Once I hear her climb the stairs to the second floor, I

can't hold back any longer. "Hello, down there! Good first day at work?"

The light pounding of her feet stops. "Hello, yourself! It was a clumsily perfect first day. Thank you for asking."

I rub the back of my hand over my lips. "Clumsily perfect? That's not a descriptor I'm familiar with. Care to elaborate?"

"Absolutely. Give me a minute to change and then I'll be right up."

The smile on my face could probably be seen from outer space. Anticipation makes me antsy, and I rise to my feet, busying myself with a stack of books that needs reshelving. Within a few moments, I sense I'm no longer alone in the room. I didn't hear her come up, but I didn't need to. She brings a sense of peace with her; it settles over the space like a warm mist on a sultry summer day. The urge to turn around and look at her is so strong that I nearly shove the last few books on the shelf. But instead, I force myself to finish what I started. Because the anticipation—the very thing that nearly drove me mad just minutes ago—feels like a heady drug. I need it in my system, but prolonging it is half the fun.

nine

DARCY

His back is to me, and I watch with rapt attention as the muscles beneath his shirt stretch and ripple with each reach of his arm. He's holding a stack of books and sliding them one by one on the shelf. There's a meticulous method to organizing books, and it makes me wonder. "Are you following the method that was already here, or is this your own system?"

"What's that?" he asks, turning around. When I first saw him yesterday, I barely noticed his physical appearance. I was too focused on him being, well, dead. But right now, I'm stunned by how beautiful he is. It's not a word that's often used to describe men, but it should be. His hair is a rich, dark brown with natural ribbons of light woven throughout. It's thick and lays in haphazard waves on top of his head. His eyes are deeply set and hold a world of mystery. Today they're slightly obscured by silver wire-rimmed glasses. Was he wearing those yesterday? He clears his throat, jolting me out of my stupor. "Everything okay, Darcy?" There's a slight smirk on his face, and I'm pretty sure he caught me staring. That makes me two for two today. Awesome.

"Uh-huh, sorry, I was just curious about your method of shelving is all," I say quietly.

"Oh, well, I'm not sure the owner will appreciate this, but since I've had nothing better to do, I went ahead and reorganized the entire collection."

"Really?" I muse, drifting slowly toward him. As I analyze the spines, I tug at my earlobe, unable to decipher the code. "Huh. So, not by genre."

"Nope," he confirms.

I lean in, scrutinizing carefully. "And not by author, either."

"Right again," he says, giving nothing away.

I lean back, rubbing my chin. "You got me. I can't figure it out." It pains me to admit it. I've spent more time in the last few years inside of a library than anywhere else. I thought I was familiar with all the frequently used methods, the majority being sorted first by fiction or nonfiction, followed by genre, and then author. But this—this is all sorts of willy-nilly. He's either a genius or a hack. Maybe he's both.

He tilts his head, regarding the shelf in front of him. "Every book in this attic library is organized by Jeremy."

I cross my arms in front of my chest and scowl at him. "No shit, Sherlock." I roll my eyes. "Listen, if you don't want to divulge your secrets, it's fine. It doesn't matter to me either way." It totally does. If he has some special new way to sort his books, I absolutely need to know, but I can't let him see the desperation. And I know feigning indifference is the oldest trick in the book, but what other choice do I have?

Luckily, he takes the bait. "No, I mean, they're organized by Jeremy as in, I have them shelved based on my personal rating system." He must read the confusion on my face because he crosses the room, reaching up and tugging a book off the shelf. "See, this one," he says, holding up a copy of *Life of Pi*, "it was an engaging book, but it only evoked a mild reaction from me so it's over here on my maybe shelf."

"Your maybe shelf?"

He holds up a finger, rushing to another shelf across the room. "And this," he adds, lifting *The Outsiders* from its spot, "it was good, but I didn't get anything from it."

"Hold on, Jeremy. That's a great book." I'm all for differing opinions, but it's hard to understand how someone couldn't "get anything" from that story.

"It is. That's not what I meant. See," he scratches his temple, looking like he's said too much.

"Go on," I prod.

"Well, see, most of the books I've read up here are good in the classic sense of the word. They're entertaining and have been a great distraction. But a few of them reach me in a way I can't really put into words. So, I thought maybe they might be a clue about who I was. But it wasn't until I read this one." He strides over to me and reaches up to a shelf above my head. There he finds a book that he carefully pulls down and hands over to me.

"*The Time Traveler's Wife*. It's one of my favorites," I say. I still remember the first time I read it. It sucked me in completely and was one of those books I devoured like it was my last meal.

"It's one of mine too," he says softly. My eyes snap to

his. We hold each other's gaze for a beat before I blink, turning away. He clears his throat. "It was while reading this book that I had an overwhelming sensation, like I'd been given a clue. But what it means, I have no idea. After that, I started organizing the books by this method. Think of it like a rating system, only instead of signifying how much I liked the book, it's a way to measure how much of a clue I think it is."

"Interesting. So, these," I say, motioning to the shelf next to where we're standing, "are the ones that gave you the most clue vibes?"

He chuckles. "Yes. These are like the *clueyest* vibes ever."

I roll my eyes and turn toward the titles. I recognize most of them and notice something I missed during the first pass. I think I was thrown off by a few adventure books like *Into Thin Air* and *The Perfect Storm*. "Jeremy?"

"Hmm?"

"Most of these are romance books. And even the ones that aren't technically in the genre have an air of romance in them." I tap a finger on *Paper Towns*. "Do you think—" I clear the odd lump in my throat and continue. "Do you think you had a great love? Or maybe you still do?"

* * *

JEREMY

The mood in the small attic has turned serious, and I want so badly to alleviate it with humor, but the way she's looking up at me with those earnest emerald eyes, has me choosing truth instead. "I think I did, or at least I was very familiar with the word and the emotions linked to it.

Whenever I read books like this one," I say, probing the binding of Colleen Hoover's *All Your Perfects*, "it's like I'm stuck on the idea of enduring love, you know?"

She clears her throat, looking away. "I don't, actually."

"So, you're telling me you've never been in love?"

Her cheeks flush, and I want to tell her to look at me, but she keeps her gaze locked somewhere off in the distance. "I thought I was, but I know now I was wrong."

"What happened?"

She gives her head a quick shake, looking back at me momentarily before directing her attention to the shelf. "It's nothing," she dismisses me quickly. "So," she says much louder. "Have you come up with any theories?"

"Theories?" I frown, trying and failing to follow her rapid change of conversation.

"Uh-huh. Have any of these books helped you recall anything about who you were?"

"Ah," I say, scratching below my ear. "It's not like that. It's more that they seem familiar. As in, I have a sense that when I was alive, I might've been able to relate to some of the things that happen within the pages." I wave a hand toward the books. A few catch my eye, and she's right; most are romances, at least in some way.

"That's interesting. So, for instance, in a book like this one," she says, pulling *You* by Caroline Kepnes off of the shelf, "you relate to obsessive stalker tendencies?" She lifts a brow, judging me.

I close my eyes and shake my head. "That one was more about Joe's infatuation with books. And arguably, he really did love Beck."

"Right. He just had a funny way of showing it is all." She smirks.

I plunge my hands into my pockets and shrug. I'm not

used to being the subject of conversation. It feels odd. "So, tell me more about this 'clumsily perfect' day of yours."

She smiles and it's remarkable. "Okay, but I need to sit down. As it turns out, chunky heeled boots are not all that comfortable when you're on your feet most of the day. I don't know what I was thinking," she says with a roll of her eyes.

She settles into the chair, and I take my spot leaning against the narrow table across from her. She immediately launches into a detailed account of her day, and I'll admit, I'm not exactly listening to every word that comes out of her mouth as much as I'm watching how animated she's become. From the lift of her arms to the fluttering of her fingers, it's obvious she takes great pride in her work. It makes me wonder if I ever had a purpose when I was alive. It's very clear this is what she's meant to be doing. It's not until she mentions someone named Silas that I begin to pay close attention to what she's saying. There was spilled coffee and lingering looks, and I know immediately that I don't like him. Since being up in this attic, I haven't felt anything close to the emotions I've read about, but right now, I'm feeling something very close to jealousy, and it stuns me.

I have no claim to Darcy. We barely know each other, but that pales in comparison to the major issue at hand. I'm dead and she is very much alive. It's clear in the way her cheeks flush as she recalls this Silas guy's reaction to her apparent clumsiness. Although, if you ask me, he's the clumsy one. Who sneaks up on someone while they're holding a full cup of coffee?

She's explaining now how she had to change her outfit, and although she's leaving out some details, I can tell the spilled coffee made her sweater unwearable in the sense that it suddenly became too revealing. And Silas witnessed it.

"Jeremy?"

"Huh?"

"Is everything okay? You seem, I don't know, kind of annoyed. I'm babbling, aren't I? I'm sorry. It's a habit I picked up from my mom. She's always going on and on; never letting anyone else get a word in. So, when you're trying to talk to her, you find yourself doing the same thing just to be heard." She covers her mouth with her hand. "And I'm doing it again. Just tell me to shut up."

"Are you kidding?" My entire face scrunches. "If you remember, I haven't had anyone to talk to in I don't know how long. You can talk to me all day every day and I will never get tired of it. Trust me. If you go as long as I have without being spoken to, without being seen, you'll understand."

The edges of her lips turn down, and the corners of her eyes follow suit. "God, that must've been so lonely."

"It was ..." I scratch my cheek. "I want to say, frustrating, but I don't know that I'm capable of experiencing human emotions. At least, I didn't think I was."

She looks down, her eyes searching her lap. "Wow. A life devoid of emotion? That's even worse."

"Hey," I call, demanding her attention. Once I have it, I continue, "Don't feel bad for me. Whatever my existence was before you arrived, no longer matters. You're here now, and I get to listen to all the details about your day. If you asked me now how I'd describe my life, I'd say it's 'clumsily perfect.'" I wink at her. Her cheeks flush, and for just a moment, I let myself revel in being the one to cause that reaction.

Take a number, Silas.

ten

DARCY

Milly rounds the corner, finding me kneeling in front of the display table. "Darcy? Those new cushions you ordered are here. They're in some pretty large boxes. Let me get you some help."

"Oh, that's okay. I can manage."

Just then, Silas appears muscling one of the boxes. "Heard these were for you. I was just at the front desk returning a book and thought you might need some help." He grins, making twin dimples visible on his cheeks. I hadn't noticed them the other day. I was too preoccupied with feeling mortified that I doused myself in coffee and then proceeded to gape at his mouth. My face heats with the memory, and I busy myself with the books I'm arranging to hide the redness that's surely taken up residence on my cheeks.

"Uh, thanks so much, Silas, right?" I don't know why

I'm pretending like I can't remember his name. We both know I do.

"Yep," he says, popping the *p*. "And you're Darcy, right?" he asks, giving me a cheeky smile.

I chuckle. "That's me."

He places the box on the floor beside me and arcs a thumb behind toward the desk. "Let me go grab the others."

I start to protest, but he's already halfway across the room.

Milly stands there watching the whole thing like she's just tuned in to the Lifetime channel. "Whew," she says, fanning her face. "Is it hot in here or is it just him? Am I right or am I right? I'm right." She laughs, and I can't help but join in. "Well, I should be getting back. I have to get started on plans for this year's Fall Book Bash. Will you be able to host a story time?"

"Sure, that's no problem. When is it again?"

"The second of November. It starts at noon and goes until four. You can choose your time, but in the past, we've always held story time around one."

"Well, then, let's keep it at one. No sense in changing what already works." I smile and she smiles back.

"Perfect. Oh, and Darcy?" She leans in, holding a hand up against her mouth. "He *is* single, by the way," she whispers.

"Huh?" I pretend as though I don't know what she's talking about, but my racing heart says otherwise.

"Silas. He and his wife have been divorced for two years now. They share custody of Paige." She grins like the cat who caught a mouse.

I shake my head. "I have rules about fraternizing with parents." I don't, but I'm also not so sure I'm comfortable with the idea of dating one of the parents whose child attends my weekly story times.

"Poppycock," she flaps her hand. "This is a small town. If you stick to that rule, you may as well be celibate." And with that, she struts away, leaving me shell-shocked with my mouth hanging open.

Silas returns carrying another box and tells me there's one more. I don't protest when he says he'll grab it. It's nice to have the help. While he's gone, I get to work cracking open the boxes. Peering inside, I'm giddy. These cushions are perfect. I ordered them in all the colors of the rainbow and plan to fan them out on the floor in ROYGBIV order. It's only been a week, but I noticed almost immediately that some of the kiddos who attend my story times have a difficult time keeping their hands to themselves. I thought it might help for each child to have their own cushion. Time will tell if it's successful or not.

I begin unloading the boxes, plopping the cushions out onto the floor. "Those are great! Nice and bright." Silas's voice surprises me, causing me to falter as I reach into the box. I end up losing my balance and falling flat on my butt. This can't be happening. Not again. Milly can give up any hope of him finding me even remotely attractive, given that I can't seem to hide my clumsy side whenever he's around. A deep chuckle comes from behind me, followed by a quick throat clearing. "You okay? I promise I'm not trying to make a habit out of startling you."

On a sigh, I lift myself up to standing, brushing my hands off on the side of the pants I'm so grateful I wore today. At least I don't have to add underwear flashing to my list of embarrassing moments around this guy. "It's fine. I was just focused on what I was doing and didn't hear you."

I turn around to face him, and his gaze drops to my feet, slowly climbing up my body until he reaches my face.

"You're right. You do look fine," he says, holding me captive with his stare.

"So," I say, with a clap of my hands. "I better get to work. Thanks again for helping me with the boxes."

"Sure thing. Actually, I don't have anywhere to be right now. Could you use some help?" he asks with a hopeful tone.

I don't need help, not really anyway. And judging by the way he keeps looking at me and how my body reacts to it, I should definitely send him away. But instead, I hear myself say, "Sure, that would be great."

I explain my vision to Silas and he smiles wide. "That's gonna be nice."

"Yeah?" I ask, feeling like his approval matters somehow. I tell myself it's only because he's a parent, and it's important he likes the way I interact with his child. But I know there's more to it than that.

"No doubt," he says, wearing a smile that's hard to read.

With his help, we have the cushions arranged in no time. Standing back with my hands on my hips, I admire the space. A sense of accomplishment settles over me.

"Oh, Darcy!" Milly exclaims from my right. "This looks fantastic! See, I knew what I was doing when I hired you." She grips my shoulder, giving it a squeeze.

"It was definitely the right move," Silas agrees. His eyes sweep over my face as he mouths, "Definitely," one more time.

* * *

JEREMY

. . .

I never minded being up in this little attic library. It was kind of like my kingdom. I was supreme ruler of all the books, able to read and rearrange them at will. Then I met Darcy, and now I spend most of my alone time—dreaming of leaving this room.

But I have to be careful. The need I feel to be with her is nearly all-consuming. I get everything from her; validation, social interaction, and conversation. It's important that I remember she has a life. An *actual* life. Not like me, stuck up here day in and day out in a permanent purgatory.

I think that's why I've been placing so much importance on her and confusing that with infatuation. Don't get me wrong. She's beautiful. Painfully so, in fact. The beauty I've seen up here has been limited to book illustrations and covers, but I've read about it more than enough to know no one and nothing comes close to her. I'm drawn to her, not so much for her physical attributes but for her emotional ones. She connects dots for me. She reminds me of my human side, at least, the humanity I once held. Not in the sense that I have any true memories of the time I was human, just that I remember the way it feels to be human.

This past week, she's told me stories about her day with some of the simplest details, like mentioning a dog she saw holding its head out the window of a car whiles its long ears flopped in the breeze. Or a woman holding the hand of a little girl while she struggles to grasp a dripping ice cream cone. Humanity isn't only made up of the largest moments. It's more about the smaller ones. The everyday things we see, interactions we have, moments we witness —those are the truest parts of what it means to be human. And those are the things I miss the most. It's strange to miss what you can't remember, but I've learned it's not impossible.

So, now, as I sit here on the floor, rifling through some of my favorite books, I look for the mundane among the pages. The details I often overlook or skim past. Darcy has taught me how important they are. How vital simplicity is.

Today, she bursts through the door, tromping up the stairs with purpose. "There you are!" She says those words nearly every day with as much gusto as the day before. It's as if she's afraid she'll come up here one day and find me gone. Her exclamation carries so much excitement, it seems like she's rejoicing each time she sees me. I thought it was enough just to be seen and heard, but now, I realize being missed and celebrated is even better.

"Here I am." I smile up at her.

She sits down on the floor beside me with crossed legs. "What's all this?" she asks, rolling her eyes over the bevy of books.

"I was just doing some homework."

"Hmm." She nods. "Learn anything interesting?"

Everything is interesting since I met you. That's what I want to say, but I can't. "Just that every detail is important. And nothing is too small to overlook."

She hums, looking introspective. "I would agree and even go a step further to say most of us go through life waiting on the next big thing, but sometimes we're so preoccupied with what's to come, we miss out on the here and now."

"Very astute observation, Miss Darcy," I say with pride.

A rosy flush fills her face, and I swear I'll never grow tired of eliciting that reaction from her. It's so visceral and one I'm incapable of. I can mold my face in a variety of expressions; wave my arms and flex my hands; I can even stomp my feet, but I can't bring color to my skin or warmth to my chest, and I can't make a heartbeat resound in the empty cavern where an organ once thrived. I'm a hollow shell. A vessel where a soul used to live.

"You okay?" Her question catches me off guard. And her slightly narrowed eyes have me scrambling.

"Um, yeah. Sorry, I suppose I've been looking at these books for so long, I'm a bit out of tune."

"Out of tune? Are you an instrument now?" She cocks her head, studying me with challenging eyes.

I shrug. "We're all instruments. The trick is learning how to play us." I smile smugly, and she laughs.

"Listen to you, all poetic. You *have* been reading these books for too long." She reaches into her back pocket, plucking out a rectangular device. "I want to show you something," she says, tapping the screen. It comes to life and a picture of a stack of books flashes for a moment before the image changes. I watch as her fingers dance along the glass, wondering if this is one of those "smart-phones" I've read about.

She looks up to find me leaning in close, examining everything she's doing with extreme fascination. Giggling, she quickly presses a hand to her mouth. "You don't know what this is, do you?" she asks, waving the device in the air.

"Sure, I do. It's a phone, isn't it?" I hope I'm right. If I've guessed wrong, I'm going to feel incredibly daft.

"Uh-huh. It's a smartphone," she says, making me grin. See, I knew what it was. "You've probably read about them, but have you ever seen one up close before?"

I shake my head, embarrassment stitching my brows.

"Ooh, this is gonna be fun," she says.

eleven

DARCY

He's like a child; eyes wide, mouth slightly ajar. He looks to be about my age, but in so many ways, he's innocent. His memory is lost, but even that probably wouldn't help him understand newer technology. Judging by the way he dresses, in a white-collared button-down with tan trousers and dark brown suspenders, I think it's been many years since he was alive. I wonder what ended his life. Did he have a family that he left behind? Was he married? Did he have kids? He's a mystery that I'd very much like to solve.

"I'm not much of a techie." I notice him frown at the word and need to remind myself that all of this is new to him. "That just means someone who is really smart when it comes to technology, like computers and smartphones; things like that." He nods. "Anyway," I continue, "smartphones are just like a pocket computer. You can look up anything your heart desires. Think of it like having a complete set of encyclopedias always at your fingertips."

His eyes widen, but he remains quiet. "There's also a camera inside them and that's what I wanted to show you. I took pictures of the children's section in the library where I work. I've been trying to make some changes and I'm really proud of how it's coming along."

I tap on the camera icon, bringing up my most recent photos. Handing my phone over to him, I give him a short lesson on how to navigate. He holds it like he's afraid it might bite. A giggle escapes and he glares at me. "Think this is funny, do you? You try living with only books for who knows how long and see how you act when someone hands you a light up box."

"Excuse me, did you just call my phone a 'light up box'?" I start laughing and it's the kind I'm not sure will ever stop.

Jeremy doesn't join me, but he does smile, looking amused. "Go ahead and have a good laugh at my expense."

"I will," I say, between hysterics.

Once I get myself under control, I lean a little closer to him so that I can explain each picture. "See, this is where I conduct story times." He nods, and is it just my imagination, or has he turned slightly rigid? "And those," I say, pointing to the colorful cushions, "are my new sit-upons. I'm hoping it helps my kiddos not be so pokey with each other."

"Pokey?" he asks. His nose scrunches up in an adorable way.

"Yeah, they seem to have trouble keeping their hands to themselves."

"Aha," he says. He continues toggling through the photos and stops on one in particular. "Who's that?" he asks, tapping the screen over Silas. I hadn't even realized he was in the photo when I took it. But there he is, smiling up at the camera. Clearly, he knew he'd be in the shot.

"Oh, that's Silas. You know that guy I was telling you about before? The one who I ran into and spilled my coffee all over myself?"

His jaw works back and forth like he's trying to chew something, but he doesn't like the taste. "I remember," he says gruffly.

"Yeah, so, um, he helped me with the boxes that the cushions came in and then he stuck around to help me arrange them." I don't know why, but I feel like I've just come home after curfew and I'm trying to explain it away to my angry parents.

"How nice of him." His tone of voice conflicts with the words. He says, "nice" with disdain. His reaction confuses me.

"Is something wrong?"

"No," he replies, handing back my phone. There are a few more pictures he hasn't seen, but he's suddenly on his feet and moving over toward one of the shelves. I guess he's seen enough.

I stay seated a few moments, wondering what just happened. It's almost like he's jealous, but that can't be it, can it? "Is it Silas?"

As soon as I say it, Jeremy whips around, glaring at me. "Why would you ask that?"

"You're kidding, right?" I ask with a chuckle, hoping to defuse the situation. But he doesn't react. He runs a finger along the edge of the shelf, bringing up a bit of dust.

Sliding his eyes to mine, he regards me with a deep crease in his forehead. "Why on earth would I be joking?"

I deflate at the question. Something has shifted. I'm not sure what's going on, but I suddenly get the distinct feeling that I'm not welcome in this space right now. I stand, sliding my phone into my back pocket, and rush toward the stairs. I'm just about to reach the first step when it hits me. "Shit," I whisper. I turn around and find him watching me, a painful look of longing on his face. "I'm so sorry. I've been incredibly selfish. You don't want to hear about my life outside of this house because it makes you realize what you're missing."

He starts shaking his head as he moves toward me, quickly closing the gap between us. "No, don't apologize. Please. Hearing about your day is the best part of mine. Truly."

I feel a warmth in the pit of my stomach that slowly disperses throughout my body. I'm struck by the sincerity of his words but still confused by how they conflict with his reaction. "If that's true, then why did you behave that way just now?"

He glances away, sucking his bottom lip into his mouth.

* * *

JEREMY

Well, now I've gone and done it. I've let my jealous emotions get the best of me and behaved like an ass. I don't know what to tell her since I can't even explain it myself. But I need to try. She deserves that much. "I think seeing your friend made me wish I could've been there to help you today. The pictures are great and I'm happy to see them, but I can only imagine what your face must have looked like when you finished setting up the space. I just would've liked to see it in person is all."

"Hey," she says, calling my attention back to her face. Her eyes soften as they regard me with something that feels a bit like pity.

"Don't do that," I snap with more bite than I mean.

She steps back as though I just took a swing at her. "Sorry," she whispers.

"Dammit," I groan. "I'm doing this all wrong."

"Doing *what* all wrong?"

"Acting human. I'm out of practice." I shrug with a small smile. If I wasn't staring so intently at her face, I might've missed it, but I catch the corners of her mouth twitch. She isn't going to give in so easily, and she shouldn't. "Listen," I say on a sigh. "I don't know how to do this properly and I'm going to mess up along the way. Quite often, I'm afraid, but if I can, I'd like to explain." She nods, and I go on, "I've been up here alone, but now that's changed. And I'm glad. You're my friend. The only friend I have in the world, and most of the time, these visits are all that I need. But sometimes, I feel as though I want more."

Her eyes widen, and her mouth rounds, and I'm screwing this up again. I rush to explain myself. "What I mean is, I wish I could leave this room, and that feeling is a little foreign to me. And back there," I say, motioning to where we were sitting earlier, "was not the best reaction, but what you were seeing was my frustration. And for that, I'm sorry."

She gives her head a small shake. "Don't apologize for that. I've thought about you being up here so often and wondered how you could be so content with it. I know you've told me you can't leave and I'm sure I already know the answer to this, but have you tried?"

I nod. "I have. The first day I was here I wandered around the room and then naturally moved to the stairs, but it was like there was some invisible barrier I couldn't penetrate. And I tried, believe me. I even attempted to toss a book down the stairs, but it just landed at my feet."

"Huh, that's bizarre," she says, her voice trailing off. The edge of her mouth curves in a sly smile as her eyes meet mine. "What book did you throw?"

I smile wide. "*A Farewell to Arms.*"

She throws her head back with laughter. In between fits, she chokes out, "Of all the secret attic libraries in the world, I'm so glad you're in mine."

"Tell me the truth, is it just because I hate Hemingway, too?" I chuckle.

She holds up her thumb and index finger an inch apart from each other. "A little."

We laugh a bit more and then settle into a comfortable silence. Darcy clears her throat. "Would you tell me about the first day you were here?"

There isn't much to tell, but I motion for her to follow me back to where we were sitting. She does, and once we're settled, I turn to her. "I haven't thought much about it. Honestly, I haven't thought much about any day here. They've all just mostly blended together. That is, until you arrived." She smiles shyly. "It's odd. I opened my eyes, and I was sitting on that chair." I point at the chair in the corner. "I had no memory of where I'd been or who I was. All I knew was my name was Jeremy and that I was dead. It's almost as if I just materialized here."

"That's wild." She stares at the chair and then looks back at me, squinting. "And you just knew you were dead? How?"

"I wish I could explain, but it's just something I knew. It's like I was allowed to know the bare minimum of things and that was one of them."

"Interesting." She taps a finger on her chin, looking thoughtful. "Maybe there's a reason you're here," she says with a crooked smile.

"And what reason might that be?"

"Well, for starters, you're my friend. And I don't know if you know this, but I don't have friends. I never really did."

"Oh, come on. I don't believe that." Kindness radiates off of her. She's the sort of person people flock to.

"It's true!" she insists. "I've had acquaintances and people I thought were my friends," a shadow passes over her face, and I want to ask her more, but she keeps talking, "but you are the first real friend I've ever had."

"And you're mine, at least as far as I can remember." I give her a sideways smile, and she giggles.

"So, see? That's a purpose, Jeremy. Your existence isn't in vain."

I know she's only trying to make me feel better, but her words reach me on another level. She called me her first *real* friend. Only I'm not real, at least not in the human sense. And when I'm with her, I'm acutely aware I'm dead while also feeling more alive than ever. She *could* be the reason I'm here. What if it were that simple? Regardless, I vow, at that moment, to be the best friend I can be. And if that means having to deal with the likes of Silas, well, so be it.

"I don't think I finished looking through those pictures on your light up box. Care to show me?"

"I thought you'd never ask," she says, giving me an easy smile. She's about to pass her phone back to me when she stops with a gasp. A wry grin fills her face. "Know what? I have an even better idea. Hang on. I'll be right back." And with that, she's gone.

twelve

DARCY

"Here, take this," I say, holding my iPad out in front of me. Jeremy doesn't reach for it. Instead, he just stands there, eyeing it like it's a bomb that will detonate upon impact. I giggle. I can't help it. His innocence has that effect on me.

It earns me a glare. His dark eyes are framed with twin brows that slash downward. Something about this look has me take a few steps back. Not because I'm afraid of him, but because I'm afraid of the way he's making me feel.

My behavior with him has been perplexing, to say the least. I've been thinking long and hard on it, and I have a theory. Humans have notoriously let me down, especially after more recent events back home. I had people surrounding me who I thought had my back, and save for my parents, I was wrong about every one of them. Jeremy isn't human, and it makes him feel like less of a risk. I find it easier to be myself around him, knowing he won't sell me out the way others have. It also helps a bit to know that he can't go anywhere. He's here to stay. He won't bail on me. He's physically incapable of it.

But what he said earlier about feeling stuck really got to me. I can't even begin to imagine how it must feel to just exist in one room, never being able to leave. And here I am, rushing up here to share the best parts of my day with him. The parts that happen when he's in here and I'm out living my life.

I remembered shoving my iPad in between a few sweaters in my suitcase before I left. I don't use it often, preferring my phone and laptop over it, but it used to come in handy for late-night Netflix binge sessions. Jeremy isn't familiar with technology, but he's pretty quick, and I'm sure I can teach him the basics.

"I can see that you're hesitating, but you can trust me, you know?"

His forehead creases as he widens his eyes. "I trust you completely."

"Uh-huh." I nod. "Then why won't you take this?" I jut my hand holding the iPad toward him.

He takes it reluctantly, flipping it over a few times in his hands. He runs a palm over the smooth aluminum back and probes the Apple logo. "What is it?"

I grin. "Another light up box, except this one is bigger than the last one I showed you."

"Oh, I don't need this," he says, trying to hand it back to me, but I shove my hands deep inside my pockets. "Seriously, Darcy. I'm going to be hopeless with this thing."

"No, you won't. It'll be fine." I waltz further into the room, nudging my chin toward the carpet. "Come on, I'll give you a quick lesson."

"I'm afraid nothing about this will be quick," he murmurs, but follows dutifully behind me.

We sit beside each other, cross-legged on the carpet. I reach over, take the iPad from him, and flip the cover open. It lights up immediately, and a display of various icons greets us.

"These," I say, waving my hand over the screen, "are apps, which is short for applications. I've downloaded several onto this device and most probably won't interest you, but there are a few I think you'll enjoy."

He studies the screen but doesn't say anything. I can only imagine how overwhelming this must be. We have no idea how long he's been dead, but it's clear it was before any of this type of technology existed.

I continue on with my lesson, showing him how the camera works and how to navigate his way around the layout. He's particularly interested when I open up the chess app. It seems Jeremy is quite the chess player. Of course, he has no memory of when he learned to play or who he played with, but based on his skill, it's clear he's no beginner.

"I had no idea you were hiding this talent," I joke.

He grins. "Neither did I."

My eyes flit around the room and land on a small round table in the corner. "You know," I say, with a sweep of my arm, "we could put a chess set over there. I may not be at your skill level, but I can still hold my own and what I don't know … well … you could teach me." The words come out all breathy and flirtatious and it stuns me. From the look on his face, it seems to stun him as well. He takes a moment before speaking.

He clears his throat. "I'd like that." Our eyes stay locked for a beat before he redirects his attention back to the iPad. "Aside from playing a few games of chess, I'm afraid I'm not sure how much I'll use this thing."

"Oh, but you haven't seen the best part!" I tap away on the screen, and before long, I have an email address set up for him that I've linked to iMessage. I add myself to his contacts and send off a text that pings my phone. I swipe open the screen and show it to him.

"Wait. Did you just use this larger light up box to send a message to the smaller one?"

I chuckle. "Sure did. Do you know what this means?"

He smirks at me, and I swear I see a twinkle in his eyes. "Darcy, I have no earthly idea what *any* of this means. You're going to have to elaborate."

I roll my eyes. "What it *means* is you and I can send messages to each other whenever I'm not here. How great is that?"

His brow furrows. "Like pen pals?"

The words are so charming that I can't help the flush on my cheeks. "Yeah, like that. Now you don't ever have to feel alone again."

* * *

JEREMY

She's explaining to me how the messaging works, but I just keep replaying those words she said over and over in my mind.

I'll never feel alone again.

It's hard to imagine, considering before I met her, I was always alone. And even now, I soak up her company like a sponge, never knowing when I might have it again. The idea that I'll have a direct connection to her any time I want is almost more than I can handle, and yet, it's everything that I want.

"Earth to Jeremy," Darcy singsongs. "Are you even listening to me?" She cranes her neck, studying my face, and what she sees there seems to sober her. "Hey," she whispers. "I know it's a lot to take in. And if it's too much, you don't have to use this."

"No, no, I want to." I rush the words. "Sorry, I'm just trying to absorb it all. You'll have to forgive me for not being so quick on the uptake." I smile and so does she.

"Of course. I know it's a learning curve. You can take it super slow. Here," she taps the screen, bringing it back to life, "why don't you try sending me a message?" I frown and she clocks it. "Look, when you tap this space, a keyboard pops up. Use it to type something. Anything at all."

I do as she says, mulling over my words as though this moment is somehow monumental. And then it comes to me—the perfect message. I type away and hit the "send" button. In seconds, her phone lights up, and she swipes it open. Her lips press together as she fights a smile. And then she's looking at me with those emerald orbs that pull me in so deeply. "Hemingway is a hack," she reads aloud with a shake of her head, and then her eyes are back on me, a mischievous grin filling her face. "Oh, this is gonna be fun."

She has no idea.

We spend the next hour huddled together—her explaining all the functions on the device and me simply basking in her presence. I notice a clock in the right-hand corner of the screen and mention how handy it will be to know exactly what time it is. She frowns, glancing from me to the screen and around the room. "Wait, are you saying there's no clock up here?" I shake my head. "Jesus, Jeremy. Why didn't you tell me?"

I shrug. "It never occurred to me."

She looks away, and at first, I think she's irritated with me for not telling her, but when she lifts her head, the only thing I see on her face is sadness. I hate that I keep eliciting that response from her. I may be dead and stuck up here, but none of this is her fault, and if anything, she's given me all that I was lacking simply by seeing me. *Really* seeing me.

There are a thousand thoughts swirling in my head at that moment, but I choose, instead, to shift the focus, asking her what else I can do with this crazy new contraption.

"Well," she hums. "You could watch a movie."

I nod, unsure I'd ever do it. I don't know how long I've been dead, but I remember motion pictures being in existence when I was alive. Mostly because they aren't a bizarre concept to me. But the idea of putting down a book to watch a screen doesn't sit right with me now and I have a feeling it didn't when I was alive, either.

"Oh! That reminds me," she says with a snap of her fingers. "You can read on here, too!"

"Now why on earth would I ever do that?" I deadpan.

She brushes a hand along the screen, bringing up an app that she claims will give me the option to read thousands of books. But I wave my arm around the room, declaring that I already have that option.

"I think I've seen enough for today," I say as I stand and sweep my hands along my pants. I mean it as a joke, but as soon as I see her face, I wish I could take it back. She smiles, but I can feel the effort as much as I can see it. She closes the cover on the iPad and sets it on the chair.

"Well, I should go back downstairs. I've got some things

I need to do before I head to bed." The words sound sour, like she's not accustomed to lying, but I've forced her hand.

And that was an hour ago. I know because thanks to this device, I can finally tell the time. But now, as I stare at the numbers watching the time pass by, I'm beginning to wonder if maybe I was better off before. After all, time passes whether you're watching or not, and at least when I wasn't watching, I was reading or occupying myself with my thoughts and fantasies.

I can't help but wonder if maybe I offended her. She was only trying to help and I can't say I don't appreciate the effort. It will be nice to have a way to get in touch with her when she isn't up here with me.

That gives me an idea.

I tap on the message icon, and as soon as the keyboard pops up, I begin typing. I hesitate for only a moment.

And then I hit send.

A few seconds pass, but it's long enough for doubt to creep in. It's a little after ten at night. Is that too late to be messaging her? She could be trying to sleep, and now here I am, disturbing her. I snap the cover closed, feeling stupid for never having a clue how I should behave around her.

I'm about to get up and choose a book when I hear a chime. Lifting the cover, the screen lights up with a waiting message. Darcy replied, and as soon as my eyes scan the words, my lips curve. I settle onto my back, propping my head with a pillow. Something tells me it's going to be a long night.

thirteen

DARCY

I yawn for what feels like the eighty-ninth time. I stayed up way too late texting with Jeremy. A fleeting smile fills my face as I remember the exchange.

Jeremy: Have you gone to sleep?
Darcy: Not yet. Looking forward to it though. *I love sleep. My life has the tendency to fall apart when I'm awake, you know?*
Jeremy: What is happening right now? You're quoting Hemingway? Are you drunk?
Darcy: LOL
Jeremy: Now you're just sending random letters. Darcy, are you all right?
Darcy: Oh my God. *face palm emoji* LOL means Laugh Out Loud. And that's exactly what I'm doing right now. I'm surprised you can't hear me.
Jeremy: How do I send little pictures like that?

Darcy: There's a little smiley face button on the bottom of the keyboard to the left of the space bar.
Jeremy: *star eyes emoji*
Darcy: You figured it out! That was quick. *thumbs up emoji*
Jeremy: *detective emoji*
Darcy: This is all you're gonna send now, isn't it?
Jeremy: *thinking emoji* *100 emoji*

We texted for the better part of two hours and most of it was complete nonsense. It was also the most fun I've had in a long time.

I laid awake for a while after we finished messaging each other. I kept thinking about how Jeremy just materialized in the attic, and although it seems random, something tells me it's far from it. It's an old house, rich with history. It could be that he used to live there a long time ago.

Jeremy and I joked about a handbook for the dead, but maybe that's not too far off base. I mean, I don't expect there to be an actual guide, but I'm certain there are many books written on the topic. Good thing I work at a library.

Waltzing over to the computers, I pull up the inter-library catalog. Pressing my finger to my lips, I mull over where to start and try typing "afterlife" in the search bar. Several results load and I notice a few autobiographies detailing near-death experiences. But I'm not sure they'll be much help here. This is probably a waste of time, but after Jeremy told me what little he knows about his arrival in the attic library, I've felt this overwhelming need to help him.

He tells me he's content, and most of the time, that seems to be true, but sometimes he gets this faraway look on his face like he's trying to decipher what all of this means. I've tried putting myself in his shoes, but it's impossible to imagine.

"Find anything interesting?" Milly sidles up beside me, peering over my shoulder.

I didn't hear her approach and am internally chastising myself for getting caught. That's what I get for looking this up at work.

Milly leans in. "Afterlife, huh? Uh-oh, you're not having an existential crisis, are you?" She chuckles, and I force myself to join in.

"No, no, nothing like that. I, uh, had a little girl at my story time earlier who told me her pet fish died. She asked me if I thought her fish was in heaven and it left me a little tongue tied." I'm shocked by how quickly the lie falls from my lips. If there is a hell, I'm probably going there. Especially considering my track record back home.

"I see. Poor thing. Well, in these types of situations, I always say it's best to say as little as possible. After all, there are so many different beliefs and you don't want to run the risk of saying the wrong thing."

"Sound advice," I say, looking back at the search results. A title catches my eye. *What Really Happens When We Die: A Skeptics Perspective*. I'm itching to click on it, but not while Milly is still standing here. I glance up at her. "I told her death is hard, and it's okay to be sad. Then I got out a fresh box of crayons and some paper and asked her to draw me a picture of her fish. That seemed to do the trick."

Milly smiles. "See, that's why I'm so glad you're here, Darcy. You're such an asset to this town."

An asset. I'm not sure how true that is, but the first three letters are right, anyway. I suppress a chuckle and make a mental note to share my cleverness with Jeremy later.

"Thanks, Milly. I'm happy to be here." That isn't a lie. It's almost been a month since I moved here and it was one of the best decisions I've ever made. Putting physical distance between myself and what happened back home has helped put things into perspective. I'm not to blame for what transpired. I'm also not ready to talk about it, but I think I will, eventually. And that brings me to my second reason for being grateful. Jeremy. He's a true friend, and I almost forgot what they looked like.

Milly claps her hands. "Well, I better get back. Still loads to do before Fall Book Bash! Can you believe it's this weekend already?"

"I honestly can't. I'm looking forward to it, though."

"Oh, you'll love it," she croons. "Everyone comes together raising money for a good cause. This year, as you know, we've chosen to sponsor the Wheaton family. I can't wait to see the look on their faces when we present them with a check. They lost so much in the fire." She shakes her head, sadness marring her features. "I'm just glad everyone joins in so willingly when help is needed. It's the best part of this little town."

I smile at her. Her pride in Baker Hill is written all over her face. I haven't lived here very long, but it's evident how much they care for each other. I doubt they'd turn on someone over a mistake that wasn't even their fault. I bristle, thinking of back home.

Milly gives my shoulder a squeeze before walking away. She's barely made it a foot before calling out to Cliff. I hear her telling him if he's going to continue hiding out from Ethel, the least he can do is cut out some cardboard letters for the milkshake stand. Chuckling to myself, I spin back around to face the computer. With a quick click, I notice there's one copy of the book located at a neighboring library. I hesitate for only a second before requesting it. It should arrive in a few days.

I stand, feeling a little lighter. I feel really good about this book. Maybe it's naive of me, but if I can understand a bit more about what life, er, death is like for Jeremy, then I might be able to help him somehow.

My lips curve. I pluck my phone from my pocket and fire off a quick text.

Darcy: How's your day going? Anything new and exciting happening?

I watch as three little dots appear and disappear. It happens a few times and then nothing. Shit. We've had this fun back and forth going on, but maybe I pushed it too far. He's living a perpetual "Groundhog Day." Everything is always the same. I don't think I'd love being reminded of that in such a callous way.

Just as I'm about to text an apology, a message comes through.

Jeremy: Funny you should ask. I've begun a major reread of *Great Expectations*. I've always hated Miss Havisham, but I'm seeing her in a new light. It's throwing my whole day off. LOL!

A laugh bubbles out of me at the sight of the acronym. Jeremy is always more formal, even in text, and to see him adapting to modern times, even a little bit, is really comical.

Darcy: Sounds like you've got your hands full. Have fun with that. *wink emoji*

I hit send and head to the bathroom. Once I'm inside, my phone dings with an incoming message.

Jeremy: *ring emoji* *broken heart emoji*

Shaking my head, I look up, catching sight of myself in the mirror. I'm practically beaming, and I look lighter—more at ease. I let out a breath. It's just fun having another literary nerd to banter with. That's all.

* * *

JEREMY

Darcy has been talking nonstop about the Fall Book Bash since she came up here. I've barely said a word. There's a smile plastered on my face, and I've made sure to nod at all the right moments, but inside, it feels like a storm is brewing. We've had some friendly conversation off and on all day through the device she gave me, but still. Hearing about her day straight from her does something to my insides. I need to get this jealousy in check or else she's going to stop visiting me. And that's the last thing I want.

"God, listen to me, going on and on. Please tell me to shut up." She presses a hand to her face. I want to tug it away, and I almost do, but I busy my hands on the edges of the blanket Darcy brought up here to make the area "cozi-er." I couldn't bring myself to tell her I don't have a clue what "cozy" feels like. I've read so many descriptors in books about things being soft or hard or bumpy or jagged, but all I feel is density. If I hold a book, I can feel its weight, but I can only guess that the cover is smooth and the pages are brittle. It's just another one of the many ways we're different.

"Never. I could listen to you talk for hours. I already have," I say, glancing at my wrist like I'm checking a watch. She gasps, pretending to be offended, and I laugh. "I'm serious, though. I enjoy listening to you and when you get excited about something, so do I." It's the truth. Even though I'm feeling jealous of the people in her life outside of this room, I still want to hear every detail.

She smiles, turning away. "I know it gets lonely up here and I just don't want to be the cause of making you feel left out."

That's impossible. She's the *only* reason I feel left out, but it isn't her fault. I just enjoy being in her company, and sometimes, when she's animated like this, I wish I could experience life outside this room with her. "Don't worry about that. I'd love to go with you to this Book Bash, but hearing you talk about it helps me feel like I'm right there with you as you prepare for it."

"You know," she says with a sly smile. "I could always FaceTime you while I'm there so you could experience a little bit of it."

My face scrunches. "What's a FaceTime?"

She laughs. "It's like a phone call only using the light up boxes and you can see each other while you talk." She waggles her eyebrows, making me chuckle.

"Oh, I don't know. That sounds a little complicated." Also, what if, on one of these calls, I happen to see her with Silas. I'm not interested in that in the slightest, though I'll keep it to myself.

"It's really not. I'll give you a tutorial then and you'll see how easy it is."

I nod, a little unsure of how I feel about the idea. On the

one hand, it would be wonderful to feel as though I was with her, but on the other, I'm not *actually* with her, and I'm afraid it might just serve as a huge reminder of that.

"Not to change the subject, but ..." she pauses, reaching into the leather bag she brought up here. She pulls out a book I haven't seen in a few weeks. One I knew she took but somehow forgot about. "I believe you dropped this." She gives me a cheeky smile.

"Aha, I wondered where this one ran off to." I run a hand over the cover, imagining the matte print might feel soft. Out of all the books I've read up here, *What the Wind Knows* is one of my favorites. I connected with it on a very intimate level, though I couldn't tell you what that means. Right from the start, it spoke to me. The idea of traveling back to the place of your ancestors was very intriguing and the time travel and love story that ensues was completely captivating. I've always believed there might be answers within it; something to explain the depth of connection I felt. But even with the multitude of read throughs I've done, no memories have been unlocked.

"It's a favorite of mine, too," she whispers. I look up, and our eyes lock. She swallows, and my gaze follows the curve of her neck. "Actually, I love all of her books. Amy Harmon is a brilliant author."

I clear my throat and slide back, putting a bit of space between us. "That she is," I agree.

"So, tell me, is this another one of your clue books?" She juts a finger at the book in my hands.

"It is." I stand, strolling over to the shelf and sliding it back in its place. I remain there for a few moments longer, hoping she doesn't ask any more questions. I don't have the answers, and it pains me to keep telling her that. It makes me sound pitiful.

She rises and strolls across the room to a different shelf. One containing books that have one or two scenes I found interesting, but again, it's nothing I've been able to piece together. My entire existence begins and ends in this room. It's almost as if someone opened up a box containing a puzzle and tossed it in the air. All the loose pieces are the books in this room, and now it's my job to assemble them in some way that makes sense. Even if only to me.

Her hands dance along the spines as my eyes slowly sweep over her. She has a style that's uniquely her. A tan herringbone skirt wraps around her waist. It's paired with a sheer black top with gauzy sleeves, and if not for the fitted black tank top underneath, it would be completely see-through. Lace black tights encase her legs, and her feet are adorned with black lace-up boots. On anyone else, I'm not sure it would work, but on her, it makes perfect sense. Her vibrant red hair is secured in twin buns with gentle wisps framing her face. I've noticed she likes to line her eyes in dark black ink that she extends to a point slightly past the edge of her eye, and today is no exception. I'm admiring the way it widens the shape of her eyes when she looks up, catching me mid-stare. Rather than turn away, I keep my gaze on hers.

She smiles and it's bright and beautiful. "Jeremy," she scolds. "You know it's rude to stare." There's a playful tone in her voice and a light dancing in her eyes.

"Is it now?" I smirk. She continues perusing the shelves, biting at her lip to contain her amusement.

"Darcy?"

"Hmm," she answers, never looking up.

"How old are you?" I blurt out the question and wish I could take it back. "You don't have to answer that. It was rude of me to ask." Now it's my turn to look away.

"It's okay. It's not like it's some big secret or anything. I'm twenty-six."

I frown. There's something about that number, but just like every other "clue," I can't put my finger on it. It's just another thing that elicited an involuntary response, with no other information as to why.

"Uh-oh, is there a problem?" she asks. Her face twists in a grimace.

"No, sorry. It's just that number. Twenty-six. It feels significant, only I have no idea why." I groan, scrubbing a hand over my face.

"God, it must be so frustrating." She paces the room a few times before stopping and looking up at me. "I wasn't going to say anything, but I requested a book from another library. It's about death and dying and it's from a skeptic's perspective." She watches me for any reaction and what she finds on my face causes her to backpedal. "I've over-stepped, haven't I? Shit. I wanted to help you, but I should've talked to you first. I just—"

"No, no. I'm not mad," I say, keeping my voice even. "You said you wanted to help me, but ... help me how exactly?"

"Well," she says with a grin, "that's something we can figure out together."

The only word I caught was *together*. I like it. I like it entirely too much.

fourteen

DARCY

It's a slow day at the library, so I'm using my time to prepare my art supplies for the Book Bash this weekend. I think I have enough construction paper, but I'm afraid I might be a little short on scissors. I know there's another box in the supply closet.

For a small library, this closet is massive. A half dozen metal shelving units are arranged in rows with plenty of room to walk through. I locate the shelf labeled "Art Supplies," and quickly find a small box of children's scissors. Before I turn to leave, a plastic bin on the shelf below catches my eye. A piece of masking tape with the word "Projector" in black ink has been crookedly affixed to the front. Curiosity gets the better of me. I set the box of scissors on the ground and slide the projector bin out onto the floor.

Popping the lid open, I spy a small black projector that looks brand new. It's not an old variety, either. This one has a USB cable jutting out of its side, making it capable of connecting to a computer or a laptop. At that moment, a lightbulb idea flashes in my head. I stack the scissor box on top of the projector container and march out of the closet carrying both.

As I make my way to Milly's office, thoughts of Jeremy swirl around in my head. I still have no idea where he came from. And why did he end up in the attic library of the house I'm renting? Maybe if I determine when the house was built and by whom, it might provide some answers. It's a long shot, but it's worth a try. Milly might have some ideas about where I should start.

I find her sitting at her desk; an open bag of Hershey's Kisses appears to have exploded in front of her. Tiny metal-wrapped chocolates adorn the surface of her desk like polka dots. "Uh-oh," I say with a grimace. "I see you've brought out the big guns. Everything okay in here?"

She chuckles. "I think so. I have a love/hate relationship with this event, you know? It's wonderful for the library and the community, but the planning is a royal pain in my ass." She plucks a candy off of her desk, unwraps it, and pops it into her mouth. "Chocolate helps, though." She winks.

I nod in solidarity. "Chocolate *always* helps."

"So, what can I do for you? Everything all set for this weekend?" Her eyebrows lift hopefully.

"Pretty much. Just a few more finishing touches, but I plan to get it all wrapped up tomorrow." I shuffle the containers in my arms, shifting the weight from one hand to the other. Milly's eyes follow the movement.

"Whatcha got there?" she asks.

I look down at the boxes and then back up at her. "Oh, just some extra pairs of scissors for this weekend. And while I was in the supply closet, I found this projector. Would you mind if I took it home for the night? I had an idea I wanted to try."

She smiles. "Of course. That was a donation we received last year and haven't had a chance to use. I had thought it might be fun to host a family movie night here sometime. You could test it out and figure out how it works."

I grin. "My thoughts, exactly." Well, not exactly, but close enough. Turning to leave, I stop in the doorway. "I almost forgot. I wanted to ask you if you knew where I might go to find out when a house was built here in Baker Hill?"

She taps a finger to her lips and casts her gaze to the ceiling. "Hmm, I'd say you could check the microfiche at Studebaker Central Library, but that would be awfully tedious." With a snap of her fingers, her eyes zing to mine. "Oh! I know what you could do. Stop by the township building over on Elm. They have zoning maps. I'm not sure how detailed they are, but if you're just looking to find out when a house was built, it might be a good place to start."

"Perfect. Thank you." I smile at her. "Since things are pretty slow, is it okay if I head out a few minutes early? I'm not sure when the township building closes, and I'd love to stop there today if I have time."

"Sure, that's fine. If you leave now, you should have plenty of time."

"Thanks! Oh, and Milly?"

"Hmm," she says, shoving another piece of chocolate into her mouth.

"Can you put a few of those aside for me? I have a feeling I might need some on Saturday."

"Darcy, don't you worry. There's no shortage to where these came from. I buy my chocolate in bulk." We laugh. I can still hear her chuckling to herself as I shove the double doors open and head outside.

* * *

The Baker Hill Township Building sits back from the road among a row of homes on a tree-lined street. If not for the small sign out front, I might think it was just another house. It's a compact brick Cape Cod with green shutters and a giant American flag flapping away on a pole affixed to the front porch.

From the outward appearance, I almost feel as though I should knock before entering, but it's a place of business, so I just turn the knob and push right in. Mrs. Fitz is leaning against the counter, prattling away to a woman seated behind the desk.

"You see, I keep telling 'em. You gotta keep your dog on a leash, but does he listen? No-sir-ee-bob. Damn thing pisses all over my rose bushes every morning without fail!"

The door bangs shut behind me, making me jump and halting Mrs. Fitz's tirade in its tracks. Both she and the woman behind the counter eye me curiously. I suddenly wish I could turn back time and stop here another day. It feels strange to poke around about a home I'm renting in front of the woman I'm renting it from.

"There you are!" Mrs. Fitz exclaims. "Been meanin' to stop by." She waddles toward me. "Bill says he noticed some lights on in the attic the other night." I open my mouth to explain, but she keeps right on talking. "Now I know I said that room was off-limits, but I've been thinking. You work at a library, so I'm guessin' you know your way around books. I'm sure you're careful."

"Absolutely," I say earnestly. "And I'm sorry if—"

"Good," she says. "It's settled then. You can look after Karen's books for her since she traded them in on that good for nothin' Ralph. Still hopin' she comes to her senses, but in the meantime, feel free to read any of her books so long as you take care of them and maybe give that room a good dusting every so often."

I nod. "I'd be happy to. And thank you for being so understanding." She purses her lips and dips her head a few times. "It's an incredible collection. Karen really has an eye for books."

Mrs. Fitz beams with pride. "That she does. It was that attic library that sold her on the house. It was only a few shelves at the time, but the room is what inspired her. She started going to yard sales and traveled all over the state to library sales. Even used that place on the computer—e somethin' or other—to buy used books from people."

I smile. "Well, she certainly knew what she was looking for."

"You heading out, Ella?" the woman behind the counter calls out.

Mrs. Fitz cranes her neck to look back. "I should probably get back to Bill. I'm sure he's starvin' to death by now." She cackles. "You take care, Ruth. And see if you can't do something about Jim's godforsaken dog."

Ruth nods. "Will do."

Mrs. Fitz pats my arm as she sidles past me. Once she's gone and out of earshot, I make my way over the counter. "Hello! Ruth, is it?"

Ruth smiles. "Yes. And you must be Darcy." She must notice my surprise because she continues, "Word travels fast in a small town."

I chuckle. "It does and I keep forgetting that."

"How can I help you, Darcy?"

I explain why I'm there, and she quickly retrieves a zoning map. Together we find the house, and I learn that it was built in 1939 by someone named Aaron Wentling. I thank Ruth for her time and leave the township building feeling a little disappointed. I'm not sure what I was expecting. Maybe I thought I'd see Jeremy's name somewhere—something to help connect him to the house. But I'm not any better off than I was before.

When I reach my car, I spy the box in the back seat and smile. The plans I have for tonight are a much-needed distraction.

* * *

JEREMY

Darcy bursts through the door like a rocket. She races up the steps carrying a bin, and when she reaches the top, her eyes scan the room with frantic exhilaration. When they land on me, the smile that fills her face would steal my breath away if I had any breath to steal.

"What's got you so excited?" I ask.

"I have a fun plan for us tonight," she croons. I feel something akin to a zing whip through my body at those words, and I don't know how to respond. Thankfully, I don't need to. She strides through the room, depositing the bin along the back wall. "This spot will be perfect for the screen."

"Screen?"

"Uh-huh." She nods. "We're going to have a movie night." She claps her hands and lets out a squeal.

Her energy is contagious, and I chuckle. "How can I help?"

Together, we hang up a white sheet along the far right wall of the attic. Darcy pulls a black box out of the bin she carried up here and plugs it into an electrical outlet. She untangles some wires as she explains that the black box is called a projector, and she's planning to connect it to her portable computer. Somehow, a movie will play and will be projected onto the white sheet. None of it makes any sense to me, but I have no doubt that Darcy knows what she's doing.

A few minutes later, we are sitting on a blanket watching a movie she calls "*Beetlejuice.*"

"This is the movie I've been quoting. You're gonna love it." She grins, and it feels like the sun, or at least what I think the sun might feel like.

Darcy's attention is fixed on the screen while mine is fixed on her. I watch the way her eyes crinkle when she thinks something's funny or how her mouth moves of its own accord, whispering the lines along with the actors in the film. Early on, when we come to the part where the Maitlands discover the handbook, Darcy leans in, whispering, "This is the book I was telling you about. Don't you wish you could just reach through the screen and grab it?"

The truth? I don't wish that at all. I might have when Darcy and I first met, but now it feels unnecessary. When I don't answer, she looks over at me, tilting her head. "Wouldn't you like to sneak a peek at it? I know I would."

I lift my shoulder in a half shrug. "I'd like to think you and I are writing our handbook."

Her lip quirks and she nods. "Yeah, I guess we are."

We watch the rest of the movie in comfortable silence. I alternate between admiring Darcy and watching the way the dusty air seems to swirl in the beam of light coming out of the projector. I picture that dense fog settling over this room, blanketing us in our own little cocoon.

The movie ends with the dead and the living co-existing as a pseudo-family. When the credits roll, we stay frozen for a moment. Neither one of us speaks. I feel her eyes on me, and I turn to face her. Something passes between us. It feels like a conversation though we never utter a word. I know this movie choice was meant to be light and entertaining, but it's suddenly become so much more.

My mind is perpetually filled with questions, but now there's a new one. And it's standing front and center.

Can the living and the dead really co-exist?

DARCY

"There, that ought to do it," I whisper, stepping back to admire my work. I've been putting together a display for a new reading incentive program I'm starting and I think it's finally finished. And just in the nick of time, too. The Fall Book Bash is tomorrow and I plan on signing up as many kiddos as I can. It's never too early to get them interested in reading.

"Miss Darcy?" A meek little voice calls from somewhere behind me.

I turn to find Paige peering up at me. "Hi-ya, sweet pea! What can I do for you?"

"Um, Miss Milly said you were reading *Skippyjon Jones* tomorrow. Can I help you?"

I drum my hand on my lip. "Hmm, let's see. Oh!" I snap my fingers. "I got it! But first, listen, Paige, this is a super important job." She watches me with a straight face and barely blinking eyes. "How good are you at clapping?"

Her eyes widen, and she proceeds to clap her hands together, loudly. "See? I'm a real good clapper."

"You sure are!" I smile at her. "Excellent! Tell you what, when I get to the clapping part in the story, you can stand and lead the group. Sound good?"

"Mm-hmm!" She bobs her head, giving me a toothless grin.

"Great! It's a deal then." I put out my fist, and she bumps hers against it.

"Uh-oh, did I just hear the word 'deal'?" Silas walks over and rests a hand on top of his daughter's head. His commanding presence fills the small space.

"Daddy! Miss Darcy is gonna let me be in charge of clapping tomorrow!" Paige exclaims.

Silas cocks his head, grinning at her. "Is she, now?" She nods emphatically. And then he's directing his attention at me. His eyes gleam and all the air in the room seems to have disappeared. "You sure you know what you're doing? This kid means business when it comes to clapping." He winks and I feel it in my stomach.

"That's what I'm counting on," I say, keeping my eyes on his even though I desperately want to look away.

He holds my gaze for a few moments longer and then leans to the side, peering past me. "What's all this?" he asks, gesturing at my display.

I suddenly feel bashful and a bit self-conscious. The idea sounded great both to me when I thought of it and to Milly when I presented it to her. But now, under the weight of Silas's intense stare, I'm second-guessing myself. My hands begin to ball into nervous fists, so I shake them out and reach for one of the sign-up forms. Handing it over to him, I launch into an explanation. "I studied early literacy in college and I guess you could say it left a mark. This is something I thought might help inspire young readers." The program encourages kids to read with their parents every day. They take home a picture that is divided up into grids. For each book they read, they color in one of the grids. Once the entire picture is colored, they bring it in to me and redeem it for a free book of their choice. I've managed to acquire some donations from a few local businesses that helped me purchase a pretty nice selection of books, if I do say so myself. I ask kids and parents to sign the initial form as a way to help hold them accountable.

"Interesting." That's it. That's all he says. And he's not wrong. It is an interesting concept, but I know what that word means to me. What does it mean to him? Is it interesting that I think it's going to work while he's certain I'll fail miserably? Is it interesting that I'm even bothering to try? I wait and watch him closely, hoping he'll add more, but he just hands the paper back to me and plunges his hands into his pockets.

My curiosity, which may or may not be morbid and self-deprecating, demands that I ask for more. I could assemble the words in any way, but for some reason, I choose to begin on the defensive. "You don't think it'll work?"

His head whips up and his forehead creases. Is that shock I see on his face or is it surprise? There's a difference. He could be shocked that I'd even think that or surprised that I'm on to him so quickly. Whatever it is, he immediately begins stammering, "I, uh, no." Now it's my turn to be shocked. He notices my response and holds up his hands. "No, that's not what I meant. It's a really nice idea."

"Nice?" Wow. He's digging a hole without even using a shovel. It's impressive.

"Yeah, nice. Um, great even. Jesus, I'm not doing the best here, am I?"

"Daddy! Father Mike says you can't use the Lord's name with veins!" Paige's eyebrows tug down in a severe V and she presses her hands to her hips.

Silas regards her with humor dancing in his eyes. "You're right, baby, except it's more like, 'don't use the Lord's name in vain.'"

She sucks her lips into her mouth. "But that doesn't make sense. You had that little vein on your head sticking out when you said Jesus's name, so see, that's why you can't say it with veins." She nods once, looking smug.

He shakes his head and looks back at me. Clearing his throat, he says, "Let me try this again. Your idea is amazing. It's the best I've heard. And I hope it works the way you think it will."

"Hope?" I ask with narrowed eyes.

"Actually, I *know* it'll work." He smiles wide and light actually gleams off of his teeth.

"Thank you." I smile back. It's kind of nice to see this side of him. The less polished, more foot in mouth, side. I was beginning to think he was inhuman, and right now, one of those is all I can handle.

Still, once I'm alone again, I snap a picture of my display and shoot it off to Jeremy with the accompanying text: "What do you think?"

His response is immediate.

Jeremy: I think it's incredible. Ingenious, really.
Nice work, Darcy. *smiley face emoji*

His praise hits me in a place that might concern me if it didn't excite me so much.

* * *

JEREMY

"Darcy, that idea is remarkable. I don't see how it could fail." She sent me a picture of an impressive colorful display she created, but I couldn't wait until she came home so I could hear more about it. The moment she came upstairs, I asked her to explain it all to me in detail.

"You really think so?" She chews on her lip. Insecurity is written all over her face. Did someone put it there?

I wish I could take her hands in mine and stop them from fidgeting. "Without a doubt." I say the words with as much conviction as I mean. "You are a true asset to that library. I hope they know that."

She immediately bursts into peals of laughter.

My face screws up in confused amusement. "What's so funny?"

She tells me a joke she came up with a little while ago involving the word asset. Well, the first three letters anyway. I chuckle, but with a bit of reservation. I'm not a fan of her putting herself down. I've had a sense that something happened in her past to make her feel less than. I don't want to pressure her, but I hope she'll talk to me when she's ready.

Her laughter dies down and a sweet smile remains. I swear I feel the warmth on my face. "Thank you. I needed to hear that."

"Why is that?"

"Hmm?" she asks, tucking a lock of copper hair behind her ear.

"You're doubting yourself. Is there a particular reason?"

We've been sitting on our blanket on the floor, but she stands now, tiptoeing around the room like she may find the answer hidden somewhere. Finally, she stops moving and turns toward me, letting her arms fall to her sides. "I don't know where it comes from or why it ever started. Actually," she pauses, thrusting a hand into her hair, "that's not entirely true. I used to believe in myself without question. It didn't matter what anyone else thought. But the thing is, Jeremy, if enough people start doubting you, it can be hard to ignore."

I rise to my feet and cross the room, stopping just in front of her. "Who's doubting you?" The words come out like a growl.

Her eyes zero in on mine, and I can read her hesitation like an old book. She wants to tell me, but she also doesn't. What part of her will win today? With a casual flap of her hand, I already know before she even speaks a word. "It's nothing. I don't know what I'm even going on about." She chuckles humorlessly.

I look away, feeling bereft. We're friends and with that comes compromise. I want her to confide in me, but I also need to respect her boundaries. If only I could give her something of mine. A deep, dark secret I've been keeping. But this isn't a level playing field. I'm a ghost with no memories.

I notice her hand move and before I even register what she's doing, she sweeps a finger along my forehead, brushing a few stray hairs aside.

Everything stops.

There is no time. No floor beneath my feet. No ceiling above my head.

My body vibrates like a string on a guitar that's just been plucked for the first time. "Do that again," I whisper.

"What?" Her voice is soft the way her hand just was.

I felt it.

"You touched me."

"Oh," she gasps. "I'm sorry. It won't happen again."

"No!" I call out, startling her, but I'm far too desperate to care. "I need it to. Right now."

"I don't understand." She starts backing away, and I reach out, encircling her wrist with my hand. Warmth radiates beneath my fingers and her pulse thrums against my skin.

"I can feel it," I rasp, my voice barely audible.

"Jeremy?" Her voice wavers, snapping me out of my fog. Fear is etched on her face, and her eyes zing between my hand around her wrist and me.

I let go, feeling the loss immediately. "Sorry, sorry," I mumble, raking my fingers at my scalp.

"What's going on?" she murmurs, looking dazed.

"It's just, well, I don't even know how to explain it."

"Please try." There's a sternness in her voice that wasn't there before. Without meaning to, I've fractured her trust. It's my need to repair it that gets me talking.

"I can't feel things." There it is. My big secret. I guess I did have one, after all.

"What does that mean, exactly?"

"It means I have no tactile response to anything I touch. I can't experience texture the way you can. If something is soft or if it's hard, I'll never know. I can't tell the difference. It's all the same to me."

"But you hold things in your hands." Her forehead wrinkles and she scratches her chin.

"That's true, but I only feel their weight. I can sense that something is in my hands, but that's where it stops. If I hold a book, I don't feel the smoothness of the pages or the round edges of the cover."

"This just keeps getting worse," she mutters, trudging

over to the chair. She plops into the seat, keeping her eyes glued to the floor.

"Worse?" Maybe I heard her wrong. I must have.

But she just nods. "Yeah, I mean, here you are stuck in this room alone where pretty much no one can see or hear you besides me. And now you tell me you can't even feel anything? God, Jeremy, that's really and truly terrible."

I move toward her with careful steps, and once I reach the chair, I kneel in front of her. "That's what I'm trying to tell you, though. It *was* terrible."

"What do you mean 'was'?" She wraps the word in air quotes.

"You just touched my forehead, and Darcy, I felt it."

I hear her sudden intake of air as her mouth falls open. "What?"

"I felt your hand. It was warm and smooth and if it's not too much to ask, I want you to do it again. I need you to. Please." I'm on my hands and knees begging her, and I don't even care. That's what desperation will do.

Her arm lifts slowly and begins to move in my direction. I close my eyes, waiting. The room is heavy with anticipation. Everything hinges on this moment. All that I thought I knew. It all changes the minute her fingers make contact with my hair. This time she runs them through the strands. Her movements are tentative at first and she stops when I gasp, but I grip her hand, urging her to continue. And when she does, I know for certain if I wasn't already dead, I would die in this spot. The feeling of Darcy's hands on me is without words. I could never describe it except to say if you try to imagine the best feeling in the world, it's only a fraction of what I'm experiencing at this moment. And as her other hand cradles my face while she continues to stroke my hair, I feel complete in a way I have never felt before.

sixteen

DARCY

"You hoo! Earth to Darcy!" Milly singsongs from my right. I jolt and look over to find her studying me, eyes filled with concern. "Hey," she says, softly. "You were a million miles away just now. Everything okay?"

I touched a ghost last night. He lives in my attic and he's my only friend and it was the single most intimate moment I've ever experienced in my life. That's what I want to say, but instead, I tell her I'm fine. "I was just thinking about how I want to arrange the little book swap table." It's more like I was *trying* to think about it. Trying and failing.

"Oh, don't waste too much of your time worrying about it. It always ends up a mess within minutes every year." She rolls her eyes and chuckles. "This looks nice, Darcy," she says, looking at my display. "You know, it looks like a good turnout for Book Bash this year. I'm sure you'll get a lot of kids signed up."

"I hope so."

She reaches out and pats my arm. It reminds me of Jeremy. I wish I was with him now instead of here at this festival. Milly seems to notice my somber mood, but she misinterprets it. "Listen, I know it's more people than you're used to at the library, but you'll be just fine. You'll mostly be dealing with kids and you're a natural with them." She gives my arm a squeeze before letting go.

I smile and murmur, "Thank you."

Once she walks away, I let myself replay the events of last night one more time. I don't know what possessed me to touch him. He looked so sad when I didn't open up about my past. I just couldn't bring myself to rehash the story. Not yet. I watched as he turned away and a lock of hair fell onto his forehead, partially obscuring his eye. I didn't even hesitate. I just reached up and swiped it out of the way. But once I did, everything changed. Jeremy's entire demeanor shifted from calm and controlled to flustered and erratic.

I had no idea he couldn't feel things. He never told me. Never let on that it was a symptom of his condition. When I think of all the times I went on and on about how warm and cozy the blanket I brought upstairs was or remarked on the softness of the chair cushion, I want to curl up and wither away. I feel like I've been rubbing life in his face.

And when I touched him ... I don't know, it's like he came alive. If I close my eyes, I can still see him kneeling before me, pleading with me to touch him again. It was as if those words entered my bloodstream and coursed through my veins, penetrating all my vital organs. I couldn't resist his request. Even now, my fingers ache to touch him again. His hair was so soft like I knew it would be. Having him that close, I let myself breathe him in. He smelled of leather and fresh ink on a warm page. He's been in the attic library for so long, he's beginning to smell like it, or maybe it smells like him.

"Ahoy there, Darcy. Need any help?"

Cliff. Milly probably sent him over to me after she ran out of things for him to do.

I feel as if I'm just waking up, and a few remnants of my dream are still holding on for dear life. Only I wasn't sleeping. And everything that happened is real. But right now, Cliff is poking around my book swap table, forcing me to push aside thoughts of my hands tangled up in Jeremy's hair. "Hi, Cliff. Um, I'm actually in pretty good shape, but I noticed they seemed to be short-handed at the bake sale table."

Cliff's eyes light up. "You don't say?" He spins around, looking out over the park, and once he spots the table, he wastes no time zooming right over. Sorry, Dianne. Looks like you're getting some help whether you want it or not.

I keep myself busy arranging books on the swap table. As I sort through the pile, a familiar title catches my eye. *A Farewell to Arms.* I smirk as I recall Jeremy telling me about how he tried to throw it down the stairs, but then I sober up, remembering how he wasn't able to. Because he's trapped.

I'm about to whip out my phone to snap a picture of it and text it to him when I'm interrupted.

"Hemingway." A deep voice observes from over my shoulder. I don't have to turn around to see who it is.

"Silas. How are you?" I sense him very close to my back, so I move to the side, putting a bit of space between us.

He grins, and is it just me, or is there something more to his smile? He looks as though he's in on a secret. "Hey, Darcy. I was trying to decide what to do when I saw you standing over here, looking absolutely beautiful in the sunlight. I don't know if I'm allowed to say that, you know, on the count of you being my daughter's librarian and all, but ... well, it's out there now." He leans against the table, looking effortlessly casual.

The compliment comes out of his mouth so naturally, yet it stuns me. He chuckles, taking my silence as flattery, though I'm not sure that's how I'm feeling. A couple of days ago, I would've been ecstatic over it, but now I just keep thinking about a ghost in suspenders with wavy hair that curls and bends around my fingers. I'm so lost in thought; it takes me a minute to realize there's a woman here talking to Silas. She thanks him profusely saying things like, "What would we do without you?" And when she walks away, he glances over at me, looking shy all of a sudden.

"What was that about?" I ask.

"Oh, that was Mrs. Seidel from the Baker Hill Foundation. They're matching all the donations received today for the Wheaton family."

"That's very generous of them." I nod, watching him closely. He tips his head once and looks away, clearly hiding something. "Okay, spill."

His head whips around. "What?"

"She was thanking you, Silas. And not in a small way, either. What are you not telling me?" I cross my arms over my chest.

"It's nothing." He shrugs. "My construction company is donating our labor to rebuild the Wheaton's home. That's all."

"That's all!" I exclaim. "You're kidding, right?" He shakes his head. "Silas! That's incredible! And she's right, you know? You deserve all the thanks and more. What an amazing thing to do." I give his arm a playful shove, and he shifts his weight onto his left leg to keep his balance.

"It's the least I could do. They have two small kids; one's the same age as Paige. That family has been through a lot. Too much. I'm happy to help." His cheeks flush.

I smile. "Well, if you're helping, then I want to help, too. I'm not the most skilled with hand tools, but I am a pretty fine painter, if I do say so myself."

"Are you now?" He smirks. "I'll keep you in mind when we get to the finishing part."

"You do that."

"Well, I should go find Paige." He looks around the park and spots her over by the swings. She's waving her arms wildly. He waves back and her resounding peals of laughter make it all the way over to us.

"Tell her to get her clapping hands ready for me."

"I will. Oh, and Darcy?"

"Hmm?"

"Put aside that Hemingway for me, will you? It's a classic." He winks, only I don't feel it this time. It falls flat. When his back is turned, I shove it off the table. It lands on the mottled grass with a small *thud*.

* * *

JEREMY

I keep trying to brush my hair aside, hoping to catch a glimpse of the feeling I had last night, but it's no use. Closing my eyes, I can still remember the warmth radiating off of her fingers as they brushed against my skin. Her blunt nails lightly scratched at my scalp as she wove her hands through my hair. My body tingled in a way I've only read about. It was like I was suspended somewhere between what I've known and what I've wanted to know. Not entirely alive, but not entirely dead, either.

I kept my eyes closed for most of the contact, but there was a moment. Right near the end. I blinked and saw her watching me with intensity. And I got the distinct feeling she didn't want to stop any more than I did. That's when I knew I wasn't alone. All the emotion I was feeling, she was feeling it too.

And then she just stopped, and I slid away. She stood, smiling, though not fully looking at me. The entire encounter suddenly felt sour and awkward. She made a bit of small talk about needing to do some laundry, and then she was gone. I was still kneeling when she left.

I've spent a good portion of the day hoping I didn't somehow screw things up. Worrying I crossed a line. I thought about sending a message to her phone several times today, but I could never come up with the right words.

The time I've spent alone with my thoughts all day has me on edge. I put my needs in front of our friendship, never once considering how they might affect Darcy. If she's feeling any discomfort, it may keep her from visiting me. God, I hope that doesn't happen.

I hear movement downstairs. I know today was the Book Bash for the library. She was up and out early this morning, but it sounds like she may be home now. All I can do is wait and hope.

I thought I might hear from her sometime today. She had mentioned something about a video call, but I'm guessing the doubts that kept me from messaging her also kept her from contacting me.

I imagine the second hand of a clock ticking away as I sit, cross-legged, on the blanket. From what I can tell, Darcy's movements are relaxed. She doesn't sound rushed as she strolls around the house. I want to call out to her. Ask her how her day was. That's what I would've done *before*. Now, it feels like the rules have changed, and I don't know what they are. Maybe she doesn't, either.

I notice a familiar sound I've grown used to—the soft scraping from whatever she props against the attic door. It's followed by a low creak as the door is pulled open. She pads up the stairs with all the casual grace of a person without a care in the world. She stands tall and treads lightly, and now I'm wondering if maybe I was wrong. Maybe I *am* all alone.

"Hey, you." She beams, crossing the room in long strides.

I suddenly wish I had thought to stand when I first heard the door open. I'm sitting on the blanket, feeling more vulnerable by the minute. But I tell myself to relax. She may not be behaving as though anything monumental happened between us, but she's also not acting angry either. "Hi. How was the big Book Bash?"

She smiles wide, and God help me, I ache to hold her. The urge is sudden and overwhelms me. I fidget on the blanket, clasping my hands behind my back. "It was great, actually. The turnout was amazing. Twenty-nine kids signed up for my young reader program. And we raised thirty-five thousand dollars for a local family who lost their home in a fire." She claps her hands and sways with excitement.

"That's incredible. Congratulations." I pat at the empty spot next to me. "Have a seat and show me pictures. Knowing you, I'm sure there are dozens."

She bites at her lip and sits down next to me. "I may have taken a few."

"Oh, you *may* have, huh?" I give her a cocky grin. "You know, I was surprised I didn't hear from you, but I'm sure you had your hands full." The words fall out of my mouth, completely unplanned.

She pauses, frowning. "Yeah, um, sorry. I guess the day got away from me." Her eyes cast down on her lap, and guilt settles over the both of us like a weighted blanket, making me wish I hadn't said anything.

"It's okay. Really. It just prolonged the excitement. I'm anxious to see pictures and hear all about it."

Darcy glances up at me. "Is that so?"

I nod, smiling wide. She smiles back and the tension in the room eases a bit.

"Well, then, far be it from me to keep you waiting." She chuckles, tugging her phone from her back pocket. She thumbs through the photos, pausing on each one to give me a small detail. This little girl had an ice cream cone that dripped all down the front of her dress. And that little boy kept shoving a finger into his nose and then right into his mouth. My face wrinkles. "Jesus, kids are repulsive."

"They are." She giggles. "But they're also amazing. So much potential and they have their whole lives ahead of them."

And there it is. It always comes back to this. Life and living. Things I can't understand. I end up feeling like an outsider, though I know it's not Darcy's intention. Without even feeling it, I know the corners of my mouth are falling. I fight to keep them up, but she notices anyway.

"Jeremy, I'm—"

"No, please don't say it," I tell her, holding a hand to her lips. They're supple and warm and I'm suddenly jealous of my own fingers. I quickly pull away, leaving her mouth parted and her breathing slightly erratic. Something indescribable happens whenever we touch. It makes me want to chase after the feeling while also running away. It's intimate in a way that seems wrong. She's alive, and I'm dead, and I need to keep reminding myself.

seventeen

DARCY

My entire body is covered in goose bumps—the good kind. The kind that happens when you're on the cusp of something amazing. But then he jerks his hand away and I feel exposed. His lips begin moving, but I'm having a hard time concentrating on what he's saying. I don't even remember what we were talking about. My mind is a jumbled mess of thoughts—*I wonder if he felt it, too*—and hopes—*touch me again, please.*

"Know what I mean?" He tilts his head expectantly. His eyes scrutinize my face. Shit. I have no idea what he said. The right corner of his mouth quirks. "You're not even listening to me, are you?" Shame washes over me. Listening is invaluable to Jeremy. No one can hear him; no one but me, that is. And now I've just been caught blatantly ignoring him. But instead of getting angry, he laughs. "Relax. All I said was the notion of being alive or dead is going to keep coming up. I don't want you feeling guilty every time you mention living. Think of it as just something you do. You read a book; you drive a car; you eat a bagel; you live your life. It's all the same."

I nod, only I'm not sure I agree. Because out of all of those things he just listed, he can only do one. It makes me wonder if he could do more. Like, if he weren't stuck in this attic library, could he have other experiences?

"Okay, now that that's settled," he says, swiping his hands together like he's brushing them free of grime. "Why don't you finish showing me the pictures?"

I don't know how he does it—shifts gears so seamlessly. I'm still reeling from his hand on my mouth. It was, in some ways, even more intimate than when my hands were in his hair last night. But I clear my throat and begin flipping through the images. There's one of Paige standing up and clapping. I snapped it fast when she was helping me with story time.

"Who's this?" Jeremy asks, tapping the screen. When he does, it enlarges just enough to bring Silas into view. He's standing slightly behind Paige, and though his face is a bit blurry, there's no missing his eyes. They aren't on his daughter. They're focused on the camera. The one I was holding.

"That's Paige. Isn't she adorable?" His head bobs and I continue. "She helped me out today. She's quite the clapper." I smile and Jeremy does, too, but it's strained.

"This guy keeps popping up. He must be a good friend. Silas, right?" Is it just me or does his voice sound tight?

"Yep, he's Paige's dad."

"Ahh, I see. She doesn't look much like him, but I can see it a little in her eyes. Is her mom in any of these pictures?" I don't miss the hopeful lift in his tone, even if it's subtle.

"I haven't actually met her yet. She and Silas are divorced, and so far, he's the only one who's brought her to story time."

"Interesting," he muses.

I press my lips together. It's clear he doesn't like Silas and I can't tell if it's because he's envious of Silas's life or if it's something else. Something I can't let myself name. Because even though he feels alive, Jeremy is dead. And we are friends. It's all we *can* be.

Still, it doesn't stop me from wanting to alleviate his jealousy a little. "Get this. Turns out, Silas loves Hemingway." I smack the sides of my face with my hands like Macaulay Culkin in *Home Alone*.

"He doesn't?" Jeremy whisper-shouts.

"He does!"

We both laugh, and Jeremy turns his attention back to the image of Paige. "Poor kid. She's lucky she has you to guide her in the right direction." It's a sweet sentiment, but it sucks all the humor out of the room. Once again, another line is drawn, dividing us. I get to leave here and have experiences. He can only live vicariously through me.

I'm itching to change the subject. "So," I say with a clap of my hands, "read any good books lately? Or ... wait ... are you still on your *Twilight* kick?"

"You say that like it's a bad thing." He glares at me, but there's a mischievous twinkle in his eyes.

I hold up my hands. "No, no. After all, you're talking to a Twihard here."

"Twihard?" He frowns.

"Uh-huh. It's a nickname for ultimate *Twilight* fans. I haven't read the books or seen the movies in a while, but I will forever be Team Edward. How about you?"

"What?"

"Are you Team Edward or Team Jacob?" I tip my chin, regarding him through narrowed eyes.

He looks away, staring off like he's looking for a way to escape this conversation. "Well, for me, there's only one logical choice for Bella." He swallows, and it strikes me as interesting since he's dead and has no reason to perform the action. It's not the first time I've witnessed him do something like that. He's scratched at his face and rubbed at his eyes. I even caught him swiping his nose with the back of his hand once. It would seem some behaviors are just inherently a part of us, even if they serve no real purpose. And when he does things like this, it's as though I'm getting to see mannerisms that were unique to him when he was alive. He swings his head back to face me, peering deep into my eyes before annihilating me on the spot. "Jacob."

My head rears back. "Jacob?"

He nods, offering no further explanation, but I can't leave well enough alone. So I ask, "Why?"

"Because he's real, Darcy. He's not some unalive, unnatural being. He's flesh and blood. Edward can only offer Bella death. Jacob can give her life." He holds my gaze like he's trying to shove the words directly into my brain. The problem is, my heart doesn't give a shit.

JEREMY

I don't know why I needed to say that. It's not like she's insinuated she wants anything more from me than friendship. But maybe I said it more for myself. Because the thoughts I've been having are not welcome and they're not fair. Not to her.

This Silas guy seems to be interested in Darcy. There's no missing the smolder in his eyes in the few pictures I've seen. And while the idea pains me more than I can say, the look she's giving me now hurts more. All of this touching is muddying the water. Where there were clear boundaries before, now there are questionable lines drawn in chalk. And I'm ready to erase them altogether. Maybe she is, too.

"So, tell me more about Silas. What's he do for a living?" I don't want the answer to that question. Anything she tells me will only make me hate him more. It all serves as a reminder that he possesses the one thing I covet most. A heartbeat. But if he's going to be the one Darcy ends up with, the least I can do is make sure he's worthy.

She sucks her bottom lip into her mouth, and I have to look away. "Well, he's pretty nice, despite the Hemingway issue." She chuckles, but I can't make myself join. "Um, he owns a construction business and, actually, he told me his team is donating their labor to help rebuild the home that was destroyed by fire."

Son of a bitch. How can I hate a guy who's doing something as selfless as building a new home for a family in need and not getting paid to do it? "That's very generous of him." It takes everything in me not to grind the words out. I keep my voice even and tone light.

"I offered to help the crew paint when they're ready," she says with a half shrug.

"Really?"

"Mm-hmm." She nods. "My parents like to keep themselves busy with house projects and they enjoy doing everything themselves. When I lived at home, I used to love helping them paint. I'm pretty skilled at cutting in. The trick is to have a very steady hand." She wears an adorable lopsided grin, looking proud of herself.

I give her an easy smile. "Huh, I can't say I've read much about painting walls in any of the books up here. There've been some stories about artists, but very little about home improvement."

She chuckles. "Yeah, I don't suppose that's a topic that makes for enthralling reading. Maybe it doesn't make for very interesting conversation, either." Her cheeks flush and she looks down at her lap.

"Nonsense. You're like a walking, talking book. You fascinate me. And I'll be honest, sometimes I'd love to skip ahead to your last page, but then I'd miss out on all the little details along the way. And that's a sacrifice I'm not willing to make." As soon as the words leave my mouth, I want to shove them back in. I just laid my cold, dead heart on the table, casually like the way you'd hand someone a tissue.

Darcy's eyes, no longer on her lap, widen as they search mine. "You really mean that?"

This is my chance. I could take it all back or explain it away, but instead, I double down. "Without a doubt."

We stare at each other in matched curiosity, each of us a mystery to the other. I wait for her to say something, but instead, she leans slightly toward me. Or is it me who's leaning? It's as if there's an invisible thread between us that's getting shorter by the second. Our faces move toward each other in a slow, synchronized dance as our eyes remain fused. I let myself wonder what it might feel like to kiss her. I shouldn't do it. Nothing good will come of it. But at this moment, I don't fucking care. Inches separate us now. As we near each other, I notice a low thrumming. It takes me a second to realize it's her heart. The steady rhythm swirls between us and I feel it inside my chest. Her heart beats loud enough for both of us.

An obnoxious alarm picks that moment to begin blaring at a deafening volume. We both jump apart. She clutches a hand to her chest, and within seconds, she's laughing. Holding up her phone, she says, "It's just my mom." She swipes at the screen and says, "Hello."

I need a little more time to recover. I may not exhibit physical signs of distress, but inside, my head is spinning. We almost kissed; at least, I'm fairly certain that's where we were heading. What would've happened if we had?

"What'd you say? Sorry, you're cutting out again. I said, 'You're cutting out again!'" Darcy's up and pacing while shouting into the phone. "Let me move to a different part of the house and call you back." She lifts her eyes to the ceiling and groans before screaming, "I'll call you back!" Then she swipes at her phone and her shoulders sag. She rolls her head toward me, a look of annoyance plastered on her face. "I need to go call her back. I've been neglecting her and I think she's seconds away from calling 911."

I nod, and a half smile tugs at my lips. "Then you better not keep her waiting."

She opens her mouth as if to say something, then snaps it shut. With a small wave, she turns, striding down the steps and out the door.

It's only after the floorboards creak as she moves down the hall that I realize I never heard her slide the barricade against the door.

eighteen

DARCY

My mom has impeccable timing. I ended up spending an hour and a half on the phone with her, reassuring her that I'm alive and well. Also, I think I may have been about to kiss the ghost who lives in my attic, though I left that part out.

I should've gone back up to talk to him, but after my mom and I hung up, I chickened out. I nearly messaged him a few times as well, but everything I wanted to say sounded trite and silly as a text message.

Last night plays over and over in my head on a loop, and in the light of day, doubt has crept in.

Why would Jeremy kiss me? I had to have imagined that. And even if I didn't, it's probably only because I'm his only point of contact. If he feels connected to me, it's out of necessity more than anything else.

"Darcy?"

I look up from the mess of finger-painted butterflies

scattered on the art table to find Milly leaning casually against a bookshelf. "Hey, Milly." I sigh.

"Those are so cute!" She juts her chin at the table.

"Yeah, they are. The kids did a great job."

She squints at me. "So why do you sound so down? Does it have anything to do with ghosts?"

My stomach plummets, and my fingers feel numb. "Why would you ask me that?" Keeping my breathing under control is nearly impossible. I *have* been thinking about ghosts—well, one in particular—but there's no way Milly would know that.

She chuckles. "This book you requested came in." She reveals the Afterlife book she had been holding behind her back.

"Oh!" I laugh, but it's forced. I didn't think it through when I ordered that, but I should've known better. This is a small town. There are no secrets here, and if there are, they don't stay hidden for long.

She studies the cover for a moment, and all I want to do is grab it out of her hands and erase this whole thing from her memory. "You've been staying in Karen Fitz's house—the one on Everly Lane, right?"

I nod, wondering where she's going with these questions.

"It's a nice little place. Been around longer than me." She eyes me carefully. "You're not worried about it being haunted, are you? Because I'm not saying I believe in any of that stuff, but I'm also not saying I don't believe, either."

"I, um, no, I don't think the house is haunted." Haunted, with its negative connotations, implies something sinister, and that isn't a word I'd use to describe Jeremy. He's more of a roommate. No, that's not right. He's a friend. That doesn't feel right, either, but it's the only name I have for what we are. "I've just always been interested in the afterlife and that book sounded right up my alley."

She nods, pulling her bottom lip into her mouth. "Well, if you ever wanted to know more, you should talk to Luna."

"Luna?"

"Mm-hmm. She lives over on South Pearl. She's what some might call *connected*." Milly must notice my confusion because she quickly adds, "To the spirit world, I mean."

"Like a psychic?"

"Shh." She spins her head around like Raegan in *The Exorcist*. Once she's satisfied that no one heard me, she looks back. Her eyes are ablaze with an intensity I've never seen from her. "Sorry," she whispers. "It's just not everyone here is as open-minded about that sort of thing. Anyway," she leans over, handing me the book, "she comes in here sometimes. Next time she's here, I'll introduce you."

I smile. "I'd like that. Thanks."

She starts to leave but then turns back. "Hey, let me know what you think of that book. If it's any good, I might want to read it after you. Never too old to learn new things, is what I always say." She winks.

Once I'm alone, I pick up the book, smoothing my hand across the cover. It has a clinical look, which isn't what I was expecting. I assumed by the title *What Really Happens When We Die: A Skeptic's Perspective*, it might be more of a memoir. Not that it matters. As long as the contents are helpful, that's all I care about.

Flipping open the cover, I notice a foreword by the author. Timothy McManon claims to have died not once, not twice, but three times. He was born with a rare blood disorder that lay dormant until he turned twenty-three. He woke up one morning with an arm swollen three times the normal size. A deadly blood clot had taken up residence in a vein in his bicep. According to his account, he flatlined three times on the operating room table within a four-hour period. Calling himself a "reformed skeptic," he asserts his unique ability to "bridge the gap" between the living and the dead.

I have to admit, as crazy as that all sounds, I'm desperate enough to hope it's true.

Scanning the table of contents, I notice a chapter called "Soul Asylum: Where do our souls go when our bodies die?". Compulsion has me snapping my fingers through the pages until I reach the section.

The library is pretty quiet at this time of day. No one's around to disturb me as I settle back onto my bottom and lean against a nearby shelf.

The first paragraph begins, "Forty-five seconds. That's how long my heart stopped beating that first time. Forty-five seconds, though it felt much longer to me. I didn't see my body on the table. I wasn't even in the operating room. I couldn't tell you where I was, but what I can say is, I was fully aware that I was dead."

That's exactly how Jeremy described it. Coincidence? Maybe. Maybe not.

I'm about to read more when I feel a tug on the sleeve of my sweater. Glancing up, I find Ben, one of the kids who often comes to my story times. "Hey there, Ben! We missed you at story time today."

"Yeah." He sniffs, rubbing the sleeve of his shirt along his nose. "My mommy had to work 'cause that dickhead told her to come in even though it's her day off." He shakes his head.

I press my lips together, trying to hold back a laugh. This is why I love working with kids. They have no filter. It's also why you need to be super careful what you say around them. A couple weeks ago, a little girl told me she saw her parents "doing a funny hug" the night before. Her poor mom turned bright red. I pretended not to hear and kept on reading.

"So, what can I help you find today, Ben? More honey bee books?"

"Nah, I've moved on to worms now."

"Oh, interesting. You know," I say, leaning in, "I think I have just the book for you."

His eyes widen. "You do?"

"I do. And this is an extra special book because it's a diary."

His little mouth rounds, and he claps with glee. Taking his hand in mine, I lead him to the section, both of us smiling. And as we stroll together, an idea begins to brew. It starts small, but as my mind turns it around, it grows like a snowball. I can't believe it never occurred to me before.

Glancing at the wall clock, I still have two hours left here. I don't know if I can wait that long.

JEREMY

"Jeremy!" Darcy calls out the moment she bursts through the front door.

The old copy of *Anna Karenina* I was flipping through falls from my hands, landing with a *thunk* at my feet.

The pound of Darcy's feet is like a drum beating louder and louder as they climb the steps. Within seconds, the attic door is yanked open. She flies up the stairs, pausing at the top to catch her breath.

Sweeping hair out of her face, she whips her head around in search of me. Once she finds me sitting on the chair, she races across the room. The soles of her boots scuff along the wood floor as she skids to a stop in front of me.

"Now that was quite the entrance. You've got me intrigued about what's to come, but I've got to be honest, I'm not sure it'll top that." I smirk at her.

"I know, not the most elegant, but listen, give me your hand." She holds hers out to me.

I stare at her outstretched hand. Her fingers reach toward me and mine twitch in my lap. It would be so easy to touch her. And after last night, it's all I've been thinking about. I wasn't sure what to expect from Darcy today. She never came back after she left to call her mom. And this morning she bolted out the door without so much as a good morning. Now she stands before me, chest heaving with labored breaths, asking me to hold her hand.

"Hey," she says softly, commanding my attention. "Do you trust me?"

"Yes," I answer without hesitation.

Her smile is brilliant. "Good. Then please just humor me and take my hand?"

Unable to deny her request, I place my hand in hers and nearly sigh from the contact. To be able to feel physical touch after going so long without it is something I don't think I'll ever get used to.

"Listen, I hate to tell you this, but I've already explored every square inch of this place." I give her a sly smile.

She swats at my arm with her free hand. "Will you stop. Just come with me."

She leads me to the top of the steps, eyeing the door at

the bottom and then glancing back at me. A look of hope dances in her eyes.

"Darcy," I say slowly. "You know I can't leave this room."

"That's the thing, Jeremy. *You* can't, but maybe *we* can."

"What are you saying?"

She lifts our entwined hands, holding them up in front of my face. "Before me, you haven't been seen or heard. You couldn't feel anything either. Maybe you've been stuck here because you just needed someone to guide you." She squeezes my hand. "I know it sounds insane, but it's worth a shot."

Is it? If it works, then sure, but Darcy wasn't here when I tried this before. I told her about throwing the Hemingway, tossing in that detail to make light of a fucking awful situation. In the days that followed, I retreated to a very dark place. I don't want to go back there again, especially not in front of her.

"I know you're nervous," she says. "I am, too, but let's try it anyway. If it doesn't work, then nothing changes, but Jeremy, what if it does?" It's the light in her eyes that convinces me.

I give her a swift nod, and she wastes no time guiding me closer to the stairs. As we near the invisible barricade, I brace for what I know is coming. Darcy will breeze right through, and I'll be held back, stopped fast like I walked into a wall. Here it comes, I think, watching her take the first step.

But it doesn't come. My feet continue to move, and suddenly, I'm past the spot. We travel down one, two, three steps before I turn my head, looking back at where we were.

"Don't look back," Darcy warns. "Just keep moving forward and whatever you do, don't let go of my hand."

I have no words. No voice to speak. Shock and awe have my throat cinched tight. I just do as she says, continuing to move while keeping my eyes forward.

It's not until we're standing in the hallway that I realize the full magnitude of what's just happened. Darcy shoves the attic door shut and leans against it, her chest heaving with each breath.

"Jeremy," she whispers. "It worked."

nineteen

DARCY

He hasn't said a word. Not since I first took him by the hand. I could sense his worry as we approached the stairs. I felt it too, but I also knew it would work. Don't ask me how. It's just a feeling I had.

I look down at our joined hands and wonder if it's safe to let go. Looking up, I find Jeremy studying them as well. His eyes find mine, and he gives me a small nod. I close my eyes and let go, fully expecting him to be back in the attic when I open them. Instead, I find him still standing before me with a look of amazement dancing over his features.

"Are you okay?" The question feels trivial given the enormity of the situation, but I ask it anyway.

His eyes wander, taking in the narrow hall. "I am, it's just, well, I thought the walls were blue for some reason," he says, staring at the muted gray plaster walls. "It's a little disappointing." He shrugs, giving me a cheeky smile.

Leave it to him to sneak in a little humor. I snicker,

shaking my head. "Then I should warn you, the rest of the house is painted a similar shade."

"I appreciate the heads-up. Gives me time to prepare myself since I assumed the downstairs was a mix of burgundy and chartreuse."

We both laugh, but his dies down as he lifts his gaze to the ceiling. He says nothing, but he doesn't have to. I know he's remembering the day we shared a conversation with me down here and him up in the attic. So much has happened since then.

I was still afraid he might come down and, well, I don't know what I thought he might do, but it was pointless to worry. He reassured me from his attic prison, and I think that's the moment I knew I needed to help him. I'm only sorry it took me so long to get here.

His head tips down and his gaze zeros in on the attic door. "You used to prop something against that." When he turns to look at me, I cast my eyes to the floor, feeling embarrassed that, what I thought was a secret, he knew all along. "I don't blame you, you know?"

"You don't?" I steal a glance and find him watching me.

He shakes his head. "No, I don't. In fact, I would've done the same."

"Somehow, I doubt that." I scoff.

"Doubt all you want. It's the truth. You had no idea how to behave around me the same way I had no clue how to act around you. But at least I knew what to expect with you being human and all. I'm a ghost. There are no guidelines where I'm concerned. All of your worries were justified." He pauses, pressing a hand to his mouth while nodding. "I can't get over how wrong we both were."

"What do you mean?"

He grins. "I had you all figured out, but you shocked me

at every turn. And you." He chuckles. "You were so unsure of me and now look at you. You're not only figuring things out; you're writing the rulebook."

I mull over his words. "I don't think I have anything figured out. I'm just really good at improvising." I smile.

"That you are." He smiles back.

"So, it's your first day out of captivity. What do you want to do?"

I barely get the words out before he answers, "I want to see where you work. Let's go to your library." His brows lift as his eyes implore mine. "What do you say?"

His answer stuns me. "You've spent the last however many days, months, maybe years in a library. Do you honestly want to go to another one?"

"Darcy," he says, stepping closer, "it's where you go when you leave here. I know the parts of you that I've seen up there." He points at the ceiling. "But there are so many aspects of you that I don't know. This is one of them. So, yes, I want to go."

My face warms from his words, and I have to close my eyes for a second to hold back the torrent of emotion I feel. I've been a children's librarian for the last four years and he's the first person to ever ask to see where I work. My parents are supportive, but in the "oh, that's great, dear" kind of way. And my friends? They never truly cared enough to know me. I know that now.

"I guess I can't argue with that," I say, trying to mask my shyness.

"Okay, then, you lead and I'll follow." He splays out his hand, motioning for me to go down the stairs.

Once we're on the first floor, I give him a minute to look around. He glides from room to room, running his hand along moldings and peering out windows. He hums quietly, looking around with a wistful expression.

"So? What do you think?" I ask, breaking him out of his trance.

"Hmm?"

He looks at me with his eyes at half-mast. "You seemed like an appraiser, examining the construction, looking for splits in the wood or cracks in the glass."

He smirks. "Is that so?" He rests his hands on his waist, drawing attention to his forearms. His shirt sleeves are rolled up to his elbows and I wonder if they've always been like that. Am I just noticing it now? From the way his muscles strain, I don't know how I could've missed it. Either way, there's no missing it now. He clears his throat, and my gaze zings to his face, where I find a raised eyebrow and the hint of a smile.

"Yeah, so, uh, I guess we should go. That is, if you still want to?" I hate how unsure I sound. There's zero confidence in my tone. It's pathetic.

Jeremy crosses the room toward me and rests a hand on my shoulder. It takes everything in me not to steal another glance at his forearm. "Darcy, I told you I wanted to go, didn't I? I haven't changed my mind in the five minutes we've been down here." His smile is kind, and his touch is soothing. The frayed edge of my nerves smooths under his reassurance.

"Okay, then!" I say with a little too much enthusiasm. But a quick peek at his face tells me I'm not alone in my excitement.

He holds out his hand, and I take it in mine, lacing our fingers together.

* * *

JEREMY

I never could've predicted any of this, but I should have. That day I first saw her tiptoeing around the attic, a look of wonder in her eyes. She was different. I knew it then, but I didn't see this coming. The way she just took me by the hand and brought me down into her world, away from the room I've been stuck in for longer than I can put into words.

"Let's go." I give her hand a squeeze, reveling in the feeling of her skin against mine.

We walk hand in hand out the front door and down the few concrete steps. I look up at the house, and the same odd feeling I had coming down from the attic overwhelms me again. It's not exactly a memory; more of a familiarity. I can't put my finger on it, but seeing it in person tugs at my insides the same way some of the books upstairs have. More clues.

The winding paved walkway leads to the driveway where Darcy's little blue car is parked. She reaches into her purse for the keys, but just as we're about to walk onto the blacktop, I hit an invisible wall. It's just like the one I encountered in the attic. Our hands are tugged apart as Darcy keeps moving while I'm forced to stop.

She turns around to face me, her expression blank as her eyes drop to our disjoined hands, both hanging at our sides. "What happened? Why'd you stop?"

"Looks like there are limits to how far you can take me," I say with a sad shrug.

"No, that can't be. Give me your hand again. We can do this. It's just a fluke."

I lift my arm, but the "wall" stops me from reaching it

out to her. I'm not surprised, but Darcy twists her hands together as her eyes brim with unshed tears.

"It's not fair," she whispers on a shaky breath.

"Hey, it's okay. Come here." I open my arms and she walks right into them. No hesitation. I close my eyes, feeling her body shake with emotion. I want to tell her to save her tears. I'm holding her in my arms, her warmth reaching every part of me. No one needs to feel sorry for me right now.

"Everything all right over there?" a gruff voice calls from across the street. We turn to find the grumbly older woman leaning out her front door. I nearly forget she can't see me until I focus on her face and the way she's leering at Darcy—with more suspicion than concern.

I drop my arms even though she doesn't see them, giving Darcy a chance to straighten up and regroup. "Hi-ya, Mrs. Fitz," she calls. "I'm fine. I was going to head out, but I got some sad news and I think I'm just gonna to go back inside for a while."

Mrs. Fitz's face softens marginally. "Are you okay?" she asks again. This time with a hint of concern.

Darcy nods, giving the older woman a half-hearted smile. "I will be."

We trudge back inside, neither of us speaking. Mrs. Fitz keeps an eye on us, er, Darcy, from her perch.

Darcy slowly shuts the door and leans against it. We stand in the foyer just as we had moments ago, but the palpable excitement is gone. In its place, profound disappointment. "I'm so sorry, Jeremy. This was a mistake."

Her words backhand me across the face. I press a hand to my cheek, expecting to feel the skin raised and warm. "Why on earth would you say that?"

"Why wouldn't I?" She lifts her palms and then lets

them fall. Her arms smack against her sides. "I got your hopes up and mine. I thought you could have a life, you know? Or at least something resembling one."

"Darcy," I say softly, moving toward her. "I'm dead. There's no life to be had for me anymore. And it looks like there are rules for me even if we don't know what they are. But please don't think for one second that you've made a mistake. Look what you've given me. I'm no longer trapped in the attic, and that's all thanks to you." I grip her chin in my hand, tilting her head so she's forced to look at me.

"But what good is that? You're still trapped." Her lip quivers and I let my thumb sweep across it. It's a dangerous move, one that causes her to suck in a breath, but the sadness that was pooling in her eyes is gone. It's replaced with something new. Twin flames seem to spark deep within her pupils. They lick the fire within mine. Together we burn for each other. It happens with no words and very little action. Desire doesn't care that she has a pulse and I don't.

"I'm not trapped," I murmur, my voice haughty and rough. "You've set me free."

We lean in, our bodies drawn together like they're tired of waiting for our minds to catch up. My eyes roam her face, settling on her mouth. Perfect pouty lips beg for mine.

We're inches apart when frantic pounding on the door obliterates the moment.

twenty

DARCY

Jeremy and I jump away from each other as though we've been caught doing something we shouldn't be. I want nothing more than to get back to where we just were, but the pounding on the door is relentless.

I grip the knob, and before giving it a turn, I glance back at Jeremy. His gaze is heated as he watches me. It fills me with relief. I was afraid I may have imagined what had just happened. But it's clear I didn't. I press my lips together, remembering the way his thumb glided along my mouth.

Another knock has me groaning and jerking the door open. I'm momentarily stunned when my eyes are level with a broad chest. I look up and find a familiar face smiling down at me. "Silas? What are you doing here?"

He grimaces. "I'm sorry to show up unannounced like this, but Milly wouldn't give me your number. Said it would be a 'policy violation.'" He chuckles.

"How'd you know where I live?" I squint up at him.

"Baker Hill's a small town, Darcy," he says, giving me a shy smile.

Of course. I moved from one small town to another. I should know better. If someone new moves in, everyone knows about it before they even have their first box unpacked. "Very true." I smile. "So, what can I do for you?"

"Well, I was hoping—" he pauses, glancing over my shoulder, and for a minute, I'm sure he must see Jeremy, but then he says, "Whoa, they left the original molding in this place? Mind if I take a look? I'm kind of an architectural junkie."

"Uh, yeah, sure." I like Silas, but right now isn't the most convenient of times for him to be popping by. But what can I say? *"Now's not a good time. I was just about to make out with my friend/roommate who's also a ghost."* Yeah, that would go over *really* well.

I back up and move off to the side, allowing Silas to pass through. Unlike Mrs. Fitz, I give him plenty of room, but he still manages to brush against my chest on his way in. I'm sure it was an accident, but it still makes me feel a little uncomfortable. Especially when he doesn't acknowledge it. But maybe he's embarrassed it happened and he doesn't want to call attention to it.

He strolls right up to the molding, barely missing Jeremy with his massive arm. I look over at Jeremy and find him regarding Silas through narrowed eyes. His opinion of Silas needs no words.

Silas rubs a meaty palm along the wood, similar to the way Jeremy did though not with the same reverence. For a guy who claims to be into this sort of thing, Silas is behaving like I asked him to come and look at the wood and not the other way around.

"So, what brings you here, Silas?" I do my best to mask

my impatience. He's a nice guy. One I may have even been interested in had I not met the invisible dead guy standing next to me.

Silas looks over his shoulder, and I don't miss the way his eyes start at my feet and slink up the length of my body. When they finally land on my face, I arch a brow, but he only snickers. "Yeah, so I know you were interested in helping to paint the Wheaton house. I was planning to head over to Griffith's Hardware to pick out some colors, and I thought you might want to join me." He shrugs, and his gaze lowers to the ground, making him appear uncharacteristically nervous.

"Don't the Wheatons want to pick out their own colors?" I ask.

He shakes his head. "Actually, they said they'd rather someone else make the choices. I think they're still feeling rattled from the fire." He takes a step closer. "So, what'd you say? Want to help?"

I want to say no. Leaving the house now is the last thing I want to do. But then I think of the Wheatons and how they lost everything. Helping to choose paint colors for their donated home seems like the least I could do. "Sure, I'd love to help. Can you give me a minute? I just need to run to the bathroom quick."

"Take your time." He grins in that adorable, boyish kind of way that tells me he and I need to have a talk. One I'm not looking forward to.

"Be right back," I tell him, shooting a *follow me* look at Jeremy.

Once we're alone in the bathroom, I turn to him, whispering, "I'm sorry about that. It feels wrong to leave right now, but I—"

"It's okay," he says in a hushed tone. "I think what you're all doing for that family is incredible."

"I won't be long."

"I'll be here," he says with a cheeky grin.

As I turn to leave, he reaches out, grasping my elbow. My eyes zero in on his hand and he releases it, misinterpreting my gaze. I want to tell him what his touch does to me. How I've never felt anything quite like it. But something stops me. I flick my eyes up to his. "Be careful, okay?" he says with a tight-lipped smile.

I want him to elaborate, but there isn't time, so I tip my head and give him my best reassuring smile.

I find Silas wandering around the living room, closely examining knickknacks like they might hold a clue to something. "Ready?" I ask, startling him.

"Sure am! This place is great, by the way."

I let my eyes sweep around the space, pausing on Jeremy at the base of the stairs. "Yeah, it really is."

* * *

JEREMY

Damn it. I never should've let her leave with that ridiculous oaf. Oaf is a stupid word, but Silas is a stupid man, so it fits. Of course, I'm in here staring out the window while he's out there with her, so maybe I'm the stupid one.

Darcy strolls down the paved path toward the driveway while Silas trails her. His hand raises like he's about to rest it on the small of her back. I can't let that happen. I rap my knuckles against the glass, making Darcy spin. She peers at the window, and the look of longing in her eyes triggers my guilt. She doesn't want to be out there with him any more than I want her to.

Silas doesn't hear me, but he drops his hand quickly when Darcy turns. Maybe it was a childish move on my part, but it worked.

They continue walking to Silas's car, but he keeps his hands to himself this time. The moment Darcy steps onto the driveway, I find myself back in the attic.

"What the hell?" I say, spinning in a circle.

I'm standing at the top of the stairs. I try going back down them, but the invisible wall is back up. Huh.

I scratch the top of my head, remembering the feel of Darcy's hand as she linked it in mine and guided me out of this room. Once I was downstairs, I could move around freely without holding her hand, but I couldn't leave the property. And when Darcy left, I was banished to the attic again.

She's the link. That much is obvious, but why her? She's remarkable and beautiful and kind, but clearly, there's more. I just wish I understood the full magnitude of all of this.

And now she's gone. Out there in his company. I saw the way he looked at her, leering with clearly perverted thoughts on his brain. I only hope he doesn't try to act on them.

What if he does?

Will she see right through him and reject his advances, or will she reciprocate?

I'm not blind. I can see the appeal of a man like him. He wears his confidence like an old suit—something he has lying around that he can shrug on whenever the need arises. I'm envious and I hate myself for it.

I know I should be encouraging her to spend time with

actual living people, but when it comes down to it, I'd rather keep her all to myself. She's a gift.

And I sound like a stalker.

I press my palms to my eyes, wishing I could scrub the image of her leaving with Silas from my brain. I haven't had a lot of experience with memories, but I'm catching on fast. Turns out they aren't so easy to get rid of once they've taken up residence in your head.

Ambling toward the chair, I plunk down onto the cushion. I have no idea how long Darcy will be gone. But standing around staring at the closed attic door won't make the time go any faster.

I reach for the book on the table next to me.

twenty-one

DARCY

Our trip to the hardware store lasted longer than I thought. In addition to paint colors, Silas asked for my opinion on kitchen knobs and tile backsplash. It was actually a lot of fun helping to pick things out. Silas told me I have an eye for design, but I think he was just being nice.

Speaking of Silas, he was very respectful at the store. I didn't notice any more lingering looks. In fact, if anything, he was more preoccupied with making sure he didn't forget anything that he needed from the store.

When we were done, he drove me past the build site. I was surprised by how much progress had already been made. The foundation was poured and all the uprights were installed. Silas told me they were working quickly so the Wheatons could move back in as soon as possible. They've been living in a hotel room and with four of them plus their dog, it's been pretty cramped.

"This is really impressive, Silas."

His cheeks flush. "Thanks, but I can't take all the credit. My team has been working around the clock to get this done. They're a great group of guys. We couldn't do this without them."

"Yeah, but it's you who owns the business. Say what you want, you are spearheading this whole thing and I think it's amazing." I nudge his arm with my elbow.

"Well, thank you," he says, smiling.

We stand together a few moments longer, admiring the structure, when Silas rubs at his stomach.

"Everything okay?" I ask, eyeing him closely.

"Uh, yeah, I just realized I never ate lunch, that's all."

"Oh, that's the story of my life." I chuckle.

"Then it's settled."

"What is?" I cock my head.

"You and I are getting some food. Come on," he says, taking my hand in his. It's large and rough and nothing like Jeremy's smooth hands.

"Oh, no thank you. I appreciate it, but I should get home." Back to Jeremy and back to where we left off. I nearly flush, thinking about how close our lips were.

"I insist. You were a great help today. This is my way of repaying you. Besides, you've gotta eat anyway, right?" He flashes his teeth in a wide smile.

"It's really not necessary." I open my mouth to say more, but he casts his eyes to the ground, and the somber expression on his face stops me.

"You'd, uh, be doin' me a favor. See, Claire has Paige tonight, and it's just, I hate eating alone." The words are rushed, like he's running away from them as soon as they leave his mouth.

How can I say no to that? "Okay, then. Let's eat." I give him a warm smile and he returns it.

Silas drives us to Diabolo's, a small Italian restaurant a few miles from the Wheaton's lot. I've heard Milly talk about how great the food is here, but I've yet to try it. When I've driven past, it gave the impression of an intimate atmosphere. Not the sort of place you might visit if you were eating alone.

When we go inside, I see how right my initial impression was. It takes a second to adjust to the dimly lit interior, but once I do, I notice small round cafe tables scattered around with small votive candles dotting the center of each one. A few couples are seated at some of the tables, leaning in close. Most of them are touching in some way. A hand held here. A shoulder graze there. We've only been here for a few minutes, but already I'm beginning to think my original plan to have a talk with Silas was correct. This place is far too intimate for friends.

The hostess greets Silas by name and gives me a quick once-over. I can't quite put my finger on it, but she's almost dismissive. As though I'm one in a long line of women Silas has brought in here. Maybe that's not a fair assumption, but she doesn't look my way again and practically tosses a menu and napkin-wrapped utensils at me.

When she walks away, I clear my throat. Here goes nothing. "Wow, this place is very, um, cozy."

"Isn't it great?" Silas says, looking around with a hint of something in his eyes. If I didn't know any better, I'd say he seems almost proud.

"Do you come here often?"

"Every chance I get," he says with conviction.

Wow, he's not even trying to deny it.

"Seriously? Silas, listen, I like you, but—"

"Sy? I didn't know you were coming in today." A smooth

voice comes from behind me, interrupting my train of thought.

"Hey, Becs," Silas says warmly. And then he's on his feet, wrapping strong arms around a petite slip of a woman with waist-length golden hair. When he pulls back, I get a good look at her and nearly gasp. She's exquisite in the way a supermodel might be if you met one in the flesh.

She turns to me, giving me a show-stopping smile that seems genuine. "Dude! Please tell me this is Darcy!" She playfully smacks his chest.

"The one and only," he says with an ear-splitting grin.

"Honey, please don't be offended when I ask you this, but your hair is the most beautiful thing I've ever seen. Is it natural?" Becs leans in close, lifting a few strands of my hair as if she's trying to examine them.

"Uh, y-yeah," I stammer, shooting Silas a curious look.

"Shit," he says, smacking his palm to his forehead. "You're probably wondering who this strange woman is touching your hair." Gee, you think? All I can do is widen my eyes, silently begging him to fill me in. "Darcy, this is my sister, Becca. Becca, this is Darcy."

Becca takes my hand in hers without waiting for me to extend it. Instead of shaking it, she holds it to her chest. "Darcy, it's lovely to meet you."

"Becca owns this restaurant," Silas adds.

I nod as everything begins to click into place. Giving Becca a warm smile, I say, "It's very nice to meet you, too."

She releases my hand, and I rest it in my lap. Flexing my fingers, I think of Jeremy and wonder what he's doing now that he's no longer stuck in the attic. I long to be with him as he explores. It feels strange to be here while he's there. Wrong even.

"What'd you think?" Silas asks with an expectant look on his face.

Uh-oh. While I was busy thinking about Jeremy, it seems Becca and Silas were asking me a question. "Sorry," I say with a small shrug. "I drifted off there for a minute. What was the question?"

They both laugh. "I guess you've gotta have your head in the clouds a bit to be able to work with kids for a living, huh?" Silas asks.

It's an odd question and a bit insulting. Becca pokes him in the arm. "I think what you do is amazing," she says.

"Oh, no doubt," Silas agrees quickly. "I was only joking. Darcy knows that." He winks, but it does nothing to alleviate the weird feeling in the pit of my stomach. "Anyway," he continues, "Becs was saying she has a lasagna for two special today. How about we give it a try?"

"That sounds good, but I'm not very hungry. I wouldn't want to waste it." That and anything that includes the words "for two" is meant for couples, and Silas and I are definitely not a couple.

"Don't worry about that," Becca says with a flap of her hand. "Whatever you can't eat, Silas will." She chuckles.

I smile and nod, wishing I could leave. Becca strolls away after telling us she'll put in the order and send over some breadsticks and iced tea.

"Your sister seems nice."

Silas smiles. "She's the best. Our mom split when I was thirteen and our dad was in and out of our lives. Becs was only eighteen, but she stepped in and raised me."

"That must have been tough."

He swallows hard, answering with a quick, "Yeah." He's quiet for a moment, taking a swig of water. "So. What about you? Any brothers or sisters?"

I shake my head. "I'm an only child."

"Oh, you're one of those, huh?" he jokes.

The conversation shifts, becoming lighter and more on the surface. I'm grateful for the reprieve and actually find myself enjoying Silas's company.

He tells me about the time he tried to assemble an outdoor play set for his daughter. I laugh as he describes the catastrophic scene. It seems he's very skilled when it comes to building homes, but as for playground equipment, not so much.

We share anecdotes from our childhoods—little stories meant to make each other laugh. I tell him about the time I cut down a funny vine growing on a tree in our backyard when I was nine that turned out to be poison oak. He shares a story from when he was eight and shoved a bead up his nose. He never told anyone, and five days later, it came out in a sneeze in front of his entire second-grade class.

"So, there I was, sitting at my desk and this blue bead is just hanging there."

"Oh my God." I wheeze. "What'd you do?"

"Asked my teacher for a tissue." He shrugs and we both laugh.

When we finish our dinner, Silas leads us out the door, and I feel his hand press against my lower back. Instead of calling attention to it, I quicken my steps, making his hand fall away.

Once we're inside the car, he sits behind the wheel, but doesn't put the key in the ignition. And I know what's coming, even though I silently pray I'm wrong.

"This was fun."

"It was," I agree.

"I'd love to do it again sometime." He gazes at me with hopeful eyes.

I take a deep breath, knowing what I have to do. "That would be nice. You're a great friend, Silas."

"Friend," he says, wrinkling his nose. "Not exactly what I was going for, but hey, I'll take it."

The drive home is quiet, but not in an awkward way, and I'm glad. I like Silas, just not the way he'd like me to.

He drops me off, and we exchange thank yous and plan to connect in a few weeks once he's ready for me to help with painting.

I close the car door and it takes everything in me to walk and not run. I'm buzzing with excitement to see Jeremy and help him figure out life, er, death, outside of the attic.

twenty-two

JEREMY

"Jeremy?" Darcy calls from downstairs. Her voice sounds supercharged like she's just finished doing something amazing. Considering she was with Silas, I'm not overly anxious to hear the details.

She calls out again, and judging by the increased volume, I can tell she's in the hallway. "Up here," I yell.

Within seconds, she bursts through the door tramping up the steps like a gazelle. She scrunches her face when she finds me sitting in the chair.

"What are you doing up here? I figured you'd be milling around downstairs, investigating the contents of drawers." She snickers.

I want to fire off a witty retort; make a barb about her stashing something sketchy in her underwear drawer. But I can't find the energy. I can't even muster a smile.

I've been stuck up here for a very long time and never once felt sorry for myself. It never even occurred to me. But now that I've met her, I pity myself on a daily basis, and it fills me with shame.

"Hey," she murmurs, padding across the floor. "What's going on?"

"I learned another rule of being dead while you were gone," I tell her. This time I find a smile, though it feels more like a frown.

"Oh yeah?" She sits on the floor at my feet, gazing up at me.

"It would seem I can only leave this room when you're home. Once you're off the property, I'm relegated back to the attic."

Her face falls. "You're serious?"

"I'm afraid so."

"So, what happens exactly? Is there some invisible force that grabs you and hauls you back up here?"

An image of me being yanked up the stairs with my arms and legs flailing in the air flashes in my head, making me chuckle. "Not exactly. I'm downstairs and then I'm up here. It's like blinking. It just happens."

"Well, that kind of puts a damper on things, doesn't it?" She scratches at her chin.

"I don't know." I shrug. "It feels weird being down there without you. It's your space and I shouldn't be in it if you're not."

She shakes her head. "I don't see it that way. You're like my roommate. You should be able to move about the house freely, with or without me."

Roommate. It sounds so clinical. So cold. Is that how she sees me? As just someone she shares a living space with? Lacking any emotional connection? Have I been reading this all wrong?

"Welp, I'm home now, so how about you and I head

back downstairs. You have to be sick of these walls." She stands, glancing around. Something on my "clue" shelf catches her eye and she rushes toward it.

Tugging out an old leather-bound book I know well, she flips open the cover, gasping when she finds it hollowed. "Jeremy," she whispers. "What is this?" Reaching inside, she pulls out a small black box. She holds it with the same reverence I did when I first discovered it. Like she knows its importance before she even opens it. I found it tucked under a loose floorboard not long after I got here. It felt significant, so I moved it to a more prominent spot.

I sidle up beside her, peering over her shoulder as she cracks it open. Twin gold bands, shiny and perfect, stare up at us. "Woah, these look like—"

"Wedding bands," I finish. She looks back at me, and for a brief second, it feels like she's looked at me this way before. The vision lasts only a moment and then it's gone. I don't know what to make of it. Maybe I'm projecting. I feel a connection to her, and I don't want to be alone in it.

She probes the bands with the tip of a finger and then carefully slides one out of its holder. It's a little daintier than the other and has an intricate floral design etched into the gold. Without warning, she slips it on the ring finger of her left hand, holding it away from her so she can examine it. I feel a phantom pain in my own ring finger. A tingle that makes me wonder if I was married when I was alive.

Darcy slides the ring off her finger and the throbbing in mine stops. "I wonder who these belonged to," she muses, placing the ring back into the box and gliding the book into place on the shelf.

Nudging my shoulder with her own, she says, "Come on, you. It's time for a change of scenery."

I follow her to the top of the stairs, where she holds out

her hand. I long to take it in mine, but I'm curious. Can I leave the room if she's home or does she have to guide me?

Holding up a finger, I take a step toward the staircase and another and another until I'm moving down the stairs, unaided.

When we're both in the hallway, she grins. "Looks like we learned another rule. You can leave the room as long as I'm in the house. You don't need me to lead the way."

I smile and nod, though I feel a bit of sadness at the thought of not having a definite reason to hold her hand every day. I'm regretting my decision to try the stairs without her.

In the living room, we sit on opposite sides of the sofa. Darcy tugs a leg under herself while I stay rigid. I didn't have much time to get used to being down here before she left, but now that I'm here, I feel out of my element in a very literal sense. The attic library felt like my turf. I understood it, hell, I even organized it, putting my mark on every square inch. But down here? I don't know how to behave.

Darcy watches me closely; her eyes skirt over my face, the set of my shoulders, the clench of my jaw. "Dude, you have to relax," she says with a giggle.

I clasp and unclasp my hands in my lap. "I'm afraid I don't know how." The corner of my mouth quirks.

"For starters," she says, "you need to loosen up your arms. Here, let me help." She stands, moving until she's behind me. Taking hold of my shoulders, she begins kneading them like she's making bread, and the dough isn't cooperating. "You know, for a dead guy, you're incredibly tense."

I snicker. "I think it must come with the territory. That whole idea of the unknown? It's anxiety-inducing."

Her hands freeze, and I want to tell her to keep moving,

but it somehow feels inappropriate. "I never gave much thought to what happens when you die," she says, barely above a whisper. "I was raised in a very religious household, but most of those values haven't carried over into adulthood. Studying Sylvia Plath in college was eye-opening. Did you know she tried to take her own life at least three times before she succeeded?" Her hands twitch as a shiver passes through her and into me. "Do you ever wonder if it's only temporary?"

"If what's only temporary?"

"Life or, in your case, death. Is this really what happens when you die or is there more that you're destined for?" She sighs. "I don't know, Jeremy. Given what we know about your current situation, I hope I'm not the *best* the afterlife has to offer you." She resumes her assault on my shoulders.

I reach up, stilling her hands with mine. "Why do you feel so unworthy?"

"I-I don't," she stammers.

"You don't sound so sure of yourself." It's odd, having this conversation while not looking at each other. It reminds me of that day weeks ago after we just met. I was in the attic and Darcy was standing on the floor below me. We talked openly despite the physical separation. Now we're in the same room, but the distance feels greater somehow.

She slides her hands out from beneath mine, and as cliché as it sounds, I feel the loss in a visceral way. When we're touching, it's as if I come alive. Not in the literal sense, but it still doesn't feel any less real. My tactile senses usually fail me, but through her, I can feel texture and warmth. When she touches me, I exist, and when she lets go, I fade.

She takes a seat on the couch, only a little closer this

time. Staring into the dark fireplace, she begins speaking, and her eyes flicker as though she's watching flames only she can see. "I wasn't always this way. In fact, it was quite the opposite. I had more confidence than I knew what to do with, and I'll be honest, sometimes it was too much. *I* was too much. I was reading all the time. Studying every word so intensely, I was sure no one else in the world understood literature the way I did." She laughs without humor. "I miss that girl sometimes, though, I wouldn't change who I am now. You see, sometimes you meet people and you let them in and it's wonderful. The best thing you ever did. And other times … well … it's a mistake. I made a few too many mistakes and that's what brought me here to Baker Hill." She looks over at me; her eyes shining with unshed tears. "I've learned confidence is something you can lose, and when you do, it's pretty hard to find it again. I'm a work in progress." She half shrugs.

There's so much in what she said, and yet there's a lot missing, too. I long to hear every word, but only when she's ready to tell me. For now, I offer a warm smile. "I think you're exactly where you're meant to be. If you weren't, you would feel immense unrest. Do you?" She frowns at my question. "Feel unrest, that is?" I add.

She looks to the ceiling, absentmindedly tapping a finger to her pinched lips. She's thinking too hard, so I say, "Don't think. Just say the first thing that comes to your mind."

"Content." It jumps from her lips as though it was trapped and has been trying to escape. Her eyes widen and she nods. "Yeah, I feel content. More than I have in a long time."

"Good." I smile. "That's really good." I feel content, too. And I want to know her. I want to study her like she studied all of those books—become an expert on all things Darcy. "So, tell me, do you have any brothers or sisters?"

"Wow, it must be 'talk about siblings' day or something." She chuckles.

I cock my head. "What am I missing?"

"Oh, it's nothing. Just earlier I met Silas's sister when we went out to dinner and he was asking about siblings, too." She flaps her hand, brushing the words aside, but it's too late. I've already zeroed in on them.

She went out to dinner with him. That sounds very much like a date. And why should I care? She has a life to live and so does he. That makes them perfect for each other. I tell myself it's just because I don't trust him, but it has nothing to do with him. His beating heart makes me feel inadequate. And it's not like I can change my situation, either. I'm stuck here. Helpless.

I stand, striding over to the fireplace. As soon as I'm there, I get to work building and lighting a fire as though I've done it a million times before. "How are you doing that?" Darcy asks. She's crouched beside me. I've been so fixated on the task at hand I never heard her approach.

The fire crackles and blazes, bathing the room in a warm light. I sit on the floor with my legs bent and lean forward, resting my arms on my knees. "I have no idea. Maybe I read about it, or maybe it's something I did when I was alive." The flames fuel my inner fury. "When I was actually worth something," I spit.

"Hey," she croons, placing a hand on my forearm and leaning in close. "You're worth something now."

I look at her and nearly gasp at the way the fire dances in her eyes; the flickering light highlights her cheekbones and licks the pout of her lips. My eyes zero in on them and they part slightly. My gaze snaps to hers and I see a heat in them that mirrors my own. I start to turn away, but she stops me, resting a hand on either side of my face. Looking deep into my eyes, she says, "You are the reason I'm content, Jeremy."

It's too much. Her words. The fire. The feel of her hands. The closeness of our bodies. I can't remember anything about my life before I came here, and I have no way of knowing what will happen in the future, but right now, right here, I don't care about any of that.

This time, there are no interruptions. No knocks at the door. Nothing to stop this current of energy. We come together like we have no choice.

Our lips press against each other's, and the instant they make contact, I swear I feel a beating in my chest. A warmth in my veins. A quickening of breath.

At first, the kiss is tentative and careful. Our mouths stay closed. She's still holding my face in her hands, and when I slide mine into her hair, it's our green light to lose control. We give in. Tasting and licking. Our tongues collide and move in a rhythmic dance. She moans and it's like a volcano erupting. I wrap my arms around her waist and tug. She obliges, lifting her hips until she's positioned in my lap.

The kiss lasts for hours or maybe minutes, and when we finally pull apart, our lips are plump and bruised and we gasp. Her for air. Me for more. Our foreheads rest together, and we laugh and wonder why we waited so long.

twenty-three

DARCY

"Did you hear me? Darcy?"

I spring to attention, finding Milly standing in front of me, eyeing me curiously. God, she's always catching me deep in thought. She's probably starting to wonder if I'm losing my mind. Actually, I've been wondering that myself.

"I'm sorry, Milly. What was it you were saying?"

"I was just telling you I was going to head out and asked if you were okay locking up by yourself. But now I feel like I should apologize for startling you. I'm not trying to sneak up on you, but it seems to keep happening." She smirks.

I feel my ears heat up as my gaze sinks to my lap. "It's me who should be apologizing. I swear I'm not usually this drifty." I chuckle, hoping to cover my embarrassment.

Milly joins in. "You mean you're not one hundred percent laser focused on cutting shapes out of construction paper?" She thrusts her hand to her hip in mock annoyance.

"I guess not," I say, laughing.

"It's okay. You *are* allowed to have a life outside of the library and sometimes that life might follow you in here. And by the way your face is turning red, I'd say you've got something exciting going on." She winks.

Exciting doesn't even begin to touch it. Last night with Jeremy was the single most romantic moment I've ever experienced. It was just a kiss, but it felt more like a promise or a prelude. I've never been kissed like that before. Like I was being consumed.

"Oh my, look at you! What's his name?"

I blink up at her. "Huh?"

"Fine. Don't tell me." She rolls her eyes. "I don't even need details. I can already tell he's amazing. Whomever he is." She grins.

She's not wrong. Jeremy has a way of making me feel like I'm the only person in the world. That could be because, for him, I am, but somehow, I don't even think that matters. He could be seen and heard by everyone, and I still believe he'd make me feel this way.

I give Milly a smile as she shrugs on her coat and waves at me. "See you tomorrow," I call out.

I'm desperate to leave, too, but I have more prep work ahead of me. I open Spotify on my phone and pick out a playlist, and within minutes, I'm jamming. I'm so dialed in to what I'm doing, I barely notice my surroundings.

"Nice music," a deep voice bellows from somewhere behind me.

I whirl around, coming face-to-face with Silas. "Oh! I didn't hear you come in. And actually," I say, glancing at my watch, "we're closed." I mentally chastise myself for not locking the door.

"Well, then I'm here just in time." He grins.

I get an odd feeling in the pit of my stomach. Something

feels off and I don't know why exactly. "What do you mean by that?" I try to keep the apprehension out of my voice.

"Darcy, have you looked outside? It's pitch-black out there. I know you're a very capable woman, but I'd feel better if you let me walk you to your car. That's why I'm here. I was just driving by and noticed yours was the only car in the lot. Burning the midnight oil?" He tips his head toward the stack of construction paper shapes I've been cutting out.

I instantly feel ashamed, though he has no idea I ever doubted his intentions. "Yeah, I guess you could say that. I was trying to get a jump on things for tomorrow's story time craft."

He strides over and lowers himself to sit beside me on the floor. His size eclipses the room, making him look like a misplaced giant. The sight of him sitting cross-legged on the brightly colored carpet has me laughing. His forehead creases and the corners of his lips curve. "What's so funny?"

When I catch my breath, I tell him how out of place he looks among all these tiny things, and he just shakes his head, chuckling gruffly. "Here. Hand me a pair of scissors and some paper. Let's get these circles cut out so we can blow this joint." He smiles warmly and I almost feel guilty. Once upon a time, I would've found him irresistible. But now, my mind only swims with thoughts of a certain ghost waiting for me back home.

For the next twenty minutes, Silas and I finish cutting out shapes and are finished in no time. "Thank you for staying. You were a huge help," I say, scooping up the scraps of paper and walking them to the recycling bin. Silas follows me into the supply room.

"Whoa, this is like a mecca for craft supplies." His eyes

widen as he scans the shelves filled with bins. Each one is labeled and organized.

"It definitely is," I agree.

"So, Darcy Simon from Williams, Vermont, I did a little digging on you." His eyes dance with amusement, and the strange feeling in my gut returns. Only this time, it's worse. My insides feel like they're performing intricate acrobatics, but I keep my expression neutral and my mouth pinched. "Seems you've made quite the mark on your hometown."

"Uh-huh," I murmur. I want out of this small room, but he's blocking the doorway. I'm not sure where he's going with all of this, but I have an idea, though I really hope I'm wrong.

"Don't worry. Your secret is safe with me." He's grinning, but it's different. Before, I thought his smiles were warm and friendly. This one feels malicious and wicked.

"I don't know what you're talking about." I spit the words.

He cocks his head, studying me like I'm an exhibit. "Now, come on. You don't have to hide from me."

I look down at my watch. "Wow, it's getting late. I better get home."

"To what?" He arcs a brow. "You live alone, don't you? What's the rush?" His eyes rake over my body. I cross my arms over my chest, and he snickers.

I walk toward the door until I'm standing right in front of him. "Excuse me, please. I'd like to get past," I plead, hating the waver in my voice.

To my surprise, he backs out of the room, holding his hands in the air. "Be my guest."

I rush to the children's area to grab my purse. Stealing a glance behind me, I find him leaning casually against one of the bookshelves a few feet away. He watches me like a predator stalking its prey. I have no idea if and when he'll strike, but I don't want to take any chances, so I make sure I keep facing him while I gather my things.

Once I'm ready, I begin moving toward the exit, wondering if it actually will be this easy. I should've known better.

"You're a naughty girl, aren't you, Darcy?"

"Silas," I say evenly, "this conversation is making me uncomfortable. I think we should end it now."

His throat bobs with deep laughter. "Uncomfortable, huh? Well, what if I set up my phone? Prop it over here on one of these shelves and hit record? Would that make you feel more *comfortable*?"

His questions turn my limbs to Jell-O, causing me to fumble. I regain my footing and keep my eyes glued to his. Just a few more steps and I'll reach the door.

"I saw your video, Darcy. The one you made with that guy. 'Kinky librarian likes it rough.'"

I don't confirm a thing, but it doesn't matter. He's found me out, and in a small town, word travels fast. "Silas, please," I stammer. "I-I didn't know. Please, you can't tell anyone." I back up a few more steps.

His grin is cunning and villainous as he watches me, knowing he has me cornered. "I have no intention of telling anyone."

I let out a breath. "Thank you—"

"If," he continues, "you do something for me."

My fingers feel numb, and my jaw aches from grinding my teeth. "Like what?"

"Well, you see, the thing is, after I watched the video, it got my creative juices flowing, if you know what I mean." He smiles again, and I think I must be the worst judge of character because I never would've suspected any of this from him. "What do you say we make a little home movie of our own? Just you and me."

My feet continue to move in tiny increments until —*finally*—my heels make contact with the door. With careful precision, I glide my hands behind me until they rest on the wide handle. "I'd say you should definitely set that camera up and then you can strip down." He's nodding wildly like I'm about to give in to his fantasy. "And then you can grab your own dick and fuck yourself!" I shove the door and it flies open.

I don't wait around to find out if he's chasing me. I run like he is, frantically pushing the unlock button on my key fob until it registers my assault. I jerk the door open and launch myself inside, locking the doors immediately. When I look up, I'm shocked to find Silas still standing by the library door. He twists the lock and steps outside, shoving the door closed behind him. Then he strolls to his car like he didn't just threaten to expose me if I didn't agree to have sex with him on video. When he reaches his car, he stops at the driver's side door and looks over at me. He lifts his hand and waves while wearing his trademark boyish smile.

"To be continued," he calls out, winking.

My skin crawls. He's insane. He has to be. That's the only explanation. And so am I if I don't get the hell out of here right now.

I turn the key in the ignition and rev the engine. Within seconds, I peel out of the lot and onto the quiet streets of Baker Hill. It's not until I'm a few blocks away that the tears begin to fall, and once they start, I'm not sure they'll ever stop.

Silas will talk. He'll tell everyone. And I don't even have to guess how they'll react. I've already been through this before. They'll be repulsed by me; disgusted that they ever liked me; horrified that they trusted me with their children. It'll all be over. Another town will turn on me and what then?

As I round the corner, turning onto my street, only one thought replays over and over in my mind. Jeremy. I can't leave Jeremy.

twenty-four

JEREMY

That kiss we shared is all I can think about as I pace the confined space. I never thought of the attic library as small before, but now that I know what's outside of these walls, I feel like an animal in a cage.

Last night was beyond anything I'd ever imagined. I still can't believe it happened. I've replayed it over and over in my mind so much that I'm beginning to wonder if I dreamed the whole thing.

After the kiss, we sat so still, both of us afraid to move for fear of disturbing the moment. I've never thought of just being with a person as an intimate act, but I'm a believer now. Because sitting in quiet stillness with Darcy, our foreheads pressed together, was intimacy on a level I can barely comprehend.

We stayed connected for an impossibly long time. The light outside vanished entirely, and the room was bathed only in the warm glow of the fire. When it started to die off, we moved wordlessly. I tended to the fireplace, and Darcy closed up the house for the night. We walked up the stairs holding hands in amicable silence. When we reached the door to her bedroom, we gave each other one last lingering look and let our hands drift apart. We haven't had a conversation about my place in this house, but at night it only feels right that I retire to the attic library. One day, that might change, but I'm not going to rush a thing. Not with Darcy.

She is a clue.

The most important one.

I'm certain of it. I only wish I knew what it all meant. It's as if it's all right there in front of me, and yet I can't see a thing.

I hear the faint sound of her car petering up the driveway. If I had a heart, it would be pounding right now. I stand at the top of the steps, ready to rush down as soon as she's in the house. The front door opens and shuts and I hesitate. Maybe it isn't my place to invade her space the moment she gets home. Should I wait for her?

Pausing, I strain to hear her, but if she's moving, she isn't making a sound. A few moments later, an odd noise catches my ear. It sounds like a whimper. It's quickly followed by another and another. It sounds like she's hurt. I have to get to her.

I dash down the stairs, taking them two at a time, and burst through the door into the hall. Sprinting down the next set of steps, I pause at the bottom long enough to see Darcy crouched in front of the door. Her head is in her hands, and her back is bobbing with silent sobs. I rush to her, gathering her in my arms.

"Hey, what happened? Are you all right? Are you hurt?" I plead with her. She gasps and hiccups, unable to speak. I brush her hair out of her face and take her chin in my hand. "Talk to me."

"It's all going to end," she whispers before erupting into sobs again.

The words are ominous and make my skin crawl. "What's going to end?"

"Us. This. Everything."

She isn't making sense. I want to get to the bottom of things, but I need to help her relax first. She'll never calm down like this. With a gentle hand, I coax her to stand and remove her coat. I keep an arm slung around her and lead her to the sofa. Tugging a blanket off of a chair, I wrap it over her shoulders. She grips it with her hands, sinking into it. "Can I get you anything? Some water, maybe?"

She shakes her head and stares blankly at the spot on the floor where we sat together last night. "I'm so stupid," she says.

The word enrages me. "No. You don't get to say that about yourself."

Her eyes slide to mine. "But I am, Jeremy. I thought I could just move to a new town and wipe the slate clean. What kind of an idiot am I? You can't hide from your mistakes. The internet is forever."

I sit down beside her, taking her hands in mine. "Tell me what happened."

Her eyes close slowly and stay that way for a moment. When she opens them, I'm gutted at the pain I see in their depths. "I never wanted you to know any of this. Honestly, I thought I could pretend it never happened. And for a while, it worked. But the past always catches up with you. And tonight, mine found me with a vengeance." She grits her teeth, and I brace for the impact. "You know I left my hometown and I've told you it wasn't on the best of terms.

There's a reason for that. I dated this guy. Chris. We weren't serious. It was casual and consensual and honestly all I had time for. It was all he wanted as well, so it seemed like the perfect setup. But here's the thing, Jeremy, when things *seem* perfect, they rarely are. Turns out Chris had a thing for making videos. It's not something I would've agreed to, but he never asked, so my opinion didn't matter." A hot rage churns deep within me. I don't like this story. She takes a breath, keeping her eyes on our joined hands. I give them a squeeze urging her to continue. "You wanna know how I found out about Chris's video? I was working in the campus library at the community college at the time and I overheard whispering one day while I was stocking the shelves. It seems Chris took it upon himself to upload the video to a porn site where it was easily discovered. And in a small town, word travels fast. My reputation was destroyed."

"That son of a bitch," I spit through clenched teeth. "How can he get away with that? Did you talk to a lawyer?"

She nods. "I did, but the asshole is smart, I'll give him that. He set up the camera in my room while I was in the bathroom and during the, um, act, he made sure you couldn't see his face. So even though the hair and build matched his, there's no way to officially prove it's him in the video. And by setting the camera up in my home, it looks like I was the one who recorded it."

I look away, trying to get a hold of my anger, but she mistakes my behavior for shame. "I don't blame you if you don't want anything to do with me after hearing all of that," she mutters.

My eyes flash to hers, and I release her hands, guiding my palms to her cheeks. "Stop. You were a victim, and none of that is your fault. I'm disgusted, but not with you." She nods slightly. "Why are you bringing this up now? You said we have to end. What happened?"

"Silas." As soon as the word leaves her mouth, I want to jump out of my seat and storm outside in search of him. I don't even need to hear more. I knew there was something off about him.

"Silas knows about the video?"

She nods once.

If he knows, it probably means he saw it. Fury courses through me like a pulse. I may not be alive, but I sure as hell feel like I am. "How?"

Her eyes close again, and this time she keeps them closed while she speaks like she's afraid if she opens them, she'll have to relive everything again. "He showed up at the library tonight. I was there alone, finishing up. At first, he was helpful. We cut out shapes for tomorrow's story time craft." She laughs like she's embarrassed, and I hate Silas for making her feel this way. "Then he told me that he did some digging into my past and he found the video. I begged him not to tell anyone, and he said he wouldn't, but ..."

I run a hand through her hair and grip the back of her neck. Bringing her toward me, I rest my forehead against hers the same way we were last night. "But what?" I ask the question though I'm terrified of the answer.

She blinks her eyes open, staring straight into mine. "He wanted to make a video of his own. So, I told him to set up his camera, take off his clothes and go fuck himself before turning and running out the door."

Relief and pride fill my chest like air. "You really said that?" She nods, giving me a small smile. "How did he react?"

"That's the thing, he didn't. He never chased me. He just locked the door to the library and walked to his car like it was a regular Tuesday night. But I don't trust him, Jeremy. He's going to ruin me. I know he is." A single tear cascades down her cheek and I swipe it with my thumb.

"Then ruin him first."

Her brow furrows. "How?"

"If he's planning to tell someone about you, where do you think he'll go first?"

She's quiet for a moment. "Probably Milly, my boss at the library."

"Then beat him to the punch. Go to Milly first thing tomorrow morning and tell her everything." She opens her mouth to protest, but I keep talking. "You've been telling me all about work for the last couple of months. I may not know these people personally, but I feel like I do. And Milly? She loves you, Darcy. I know the people in your hometown let you down, but it might be different here. Give these people a chance to prove you wrong. And cut off Silas right at the source. What have you got to lose?"

"You're right," she whispers.

"Of course, I am." I smile wide and it coaxes her mouth to match mine.

"How'd you get to be so all-knowing? Your interpersonal skills are amazing for a guy who mostly communicates with fictional characters," she jokes.

I shrug. "What can I say? I'm an astute observer. Most of the characters in books are reactionary. I've learned from them; mostly I've learned from their mistakes."

She pulls back and stares at me, and for a second, I think she's going to kiss me, but instead, she wraps her arms around my neck and sinks into me. My arms envelop her, holding her close. We stay that way, and after a time, her breathing becomes even, and her body sighs against me. I angle my head and confirm what I already knew. She's asleep. Moving with care, I untangle her limbs from mine and scoop her up. I carry her up the stairs and lay her out on her bed. Lifting the covers over her, I pause, gazing at her face. As I turn to leave, she grabs my arm. "Don't go. Please, just lie with me for a while?"

I oblige, slinking under the blanket to lie next to her. She rolls onto her side, and I curve my body around hers. A soft, contented moan escapes her lips. She relaxes against me, and I wrap my arms around her, silently promising to never let go. And I don't.

twenty-five

DARCY

I awaken warm and heavy, feeling a bit hungover though I haven't had a drop to drink. It takes a moment for my eyes to adjust, and when they do, I find Jeremy staring back at me. "You're here," I say with a smile.

"I am." He rests a hand on my face, rubbing his thumb back and forth along my cheek. "Sleep well?"

"Mm-hmm. I slept like the—" I stop myself, but he's too perceptive not to notice.

"Like what?" He arcs a brow.

"Nothing. It's just a dumb saying. I don't even know why I thought of it." I direct my attention to the ceiling, fixating on a small crack in the plaster.

"Darcy? I didn't leave after you opened up to me last night, did I?"

"No," I answer, lolling my head back to face him. "You didn't." He nods expectantly. "Fine. I was just gonna say, 'I slept like the dead,' but that seemed, I don't know, disrespectful." I roll my eyes.

"Well, that's the dumbest thing I've ever heard."

My eyes widen. "Excuse me?"

He chuckles, but I don't join in, and when he notices, he groans. "Oh, come on, it's a joke. I mean, I don't sleep *at all*, so if you slept like me, then you didn't sleep."

I never knew he didn't sleep. I guess I hadn't thought about it. But now it's *all* I'm thinking about. "Did you just lie there all night and stare at me like some kind of creeper?"

"There's that word again. I thought we were past that. I'm not a creeper. I'm an admirer; a protector; a knight in shining armor, if you will." He purses his lips, trying to look distinguished.

I laugh. "Well, you're something, all right."

I let my eyes roam his face. His skin is smooth, never experiencing a five o'clock shadow. His eyes are deeply set and the skin around them wrinkles slightly. His eyebrows are thick and dark, just like his hair, which falls in unruly waves that always look sexy and tousled. To quote Maggie, an old college friend, he's "sex on a stick." We both examine each other, scrutinizing every bump, every wrinkle, every surface until he interrupts. "Shouldn't you get ready for work? No sense prolonging the inevitable."

"Do I have to?" I groan.

"I'm afraid so, but listen, it's important that you fight for yourself. Go in there and don't back down. Silas has no right to take away everything you've worked so hard for. Don't let him."

Jeremy's words sink in, dousing my insides with gasoline. It's time to light the match.

A half hour later, I'm ready to leave. He walks me to the door taking my hand in his and bringing it to his mouth. I hold my breath as he places a soft kiss on my palm. He guides my hand to rest over my heart and holds it there. "I can't be there physically, but that doesn't mean I'm not there with you."

I smile and nod, feigning confidence, and then I breeze out the door, muttering a quiet plea under my breath. "Please don't make me leave him."

* * *

I arrive at the library a half hour before it opens. Milly's car is already in the lot. I trudge toward the front door like I'm about to stand before a firing squad.

I don't even bother taking my things to the children's section. My feet take me directly to Milly's office. She looks up, smiling the way she always does. Will this be the last time she looks at me that way?

"Good morning, Milly," I say, barely recognizing my own voice.

"Hi-ya, Darcy. You're here early."

"Yeah, I, uh, wanted to talk to you if that's okay."

She nods. "Sure thing. Come on in and have a seat."

I'm grateful for the chair in her office because my legs are about two seconds away from giving out. Once I'm seated, I open my mouth to begin speaking, but Milly beats me to it.

"Is this about Silas?"

Shit. He must've gotten to her first. My body erupts in involuntary shivers. "Um, h-how did you know?" I stutter.

She's still smiling as she speaks, which strikes me as odd, though Silas did an awful lot of smiling yesterday too. Just like him, I may be misreading her demeanor altogether.

"When I got here this morning, the alarm wasn't set." In my hurry to leave, I completely forgot about the alarm. "We've been having trouble with it lately. Even though someone sets it, it doesn't always take. So, I reviewed the camera footage from last night to see if that's what happened."

"Camera footage?" I ask with a shaky voice.

"Uh-huh. We have security cameras all over the library. There was a break in about five years back. Just some high school kids, but they did quite a bit of damage. We installed the cameras shortly after, but luckily, they haven't captured much. Until now." She eyes me carefully, though her expression is unreadable.

"And, um, do the cameras pick up sound as well as video?"

She nods slowly. "They do. I heard it all, Darcy," she sighs. "Every word. And I want you to know, I don't give a damn."

"You what?" I lean back against the chair, feeling like I might collapse.

"It's like I told you last night. Everyone has a life outside of this library and as long as that life doesn't negatively impact your work in here, I don't care. I mean, I care that you're safe and well, but other than that, it doesn't matter to me."

"But Milly, did you hear what was said? Do you understand the enormity of—"

She holds up a hand. "What I heard was a disgusting man propositioning someone on my staff. A man who had no business being here after hours. A man who should know better."

I sigh at her words, but another thought pops into my head. "But what if he tells people about me?"

"So, what if he does?" She shrugs.

"Milly, you may be okay with all of this, but that doesn't mean others will."

"Unfortunately, you're right, but don't worry, I took care of it." A triumphant smile blooms on her face.

My eyes narrow. "Took care of it, how?"

"Easy. I called Silas this morning and had a little chat with him. You see, he has a bit of a reputation around here. He may be easy on the eyes, but for a small town, he's made quite the rounds. He's on thin ice with a lot of people and I let him know he better not tell anyone what he's learned about you. And if I find out he has, I will make sure this footage is slipped in to the town slideshow that plays during the Christmas bazaar." She crosses her arms over her chest, grinning proudly.

"That's amazing and all, but I don't want the town to see what happened between us."

She lays a hand over her heart and leans in. "That won't happen, Darcy. There's no need. Silas folded faster than that damn chair in the break room that collapses the moment you try and sit on it." She laughs.

I want to join her, but something holds me back. "But I'm going to have to see him again. I adore Paige, but having to interact with Silas?" A cold shiver runs down my spine.

"Another thing you no longer have to worry about," she says. "From now on, Claire, Paige's mom, is the only one welcome in the library. That was another stipulation of my deal with Silas."

Now I finally laugh. "Wow, you know, you might've missed your calling in life."

"Is that so?"

"You would've made a kick-ass attorney. I could've used you a year ago." I chuckle.

Her eyes turn serious. "I may not be a lawyer, but I think I might know someone who could help you."

"Really?"

"Mm-hmm. I'll write down their name and number for you."

"I'd appreciate that, though I'm not sure it would do much good. I've been told I don't have a case and Chris is out there living his life freely while this hangs over my head. It's a constant threat." My eyes begin to well, but I blink away the tears. I've cried enough over that asshole. From this moment on, he gets nothing more from me.

She stands, striding over to me. She places a comforting hand on my shoulder the same way my mother did when I first told her about the video. "None of this is your fault, you know?" My parents told me that, too, though my dad has never quite looked at me the same. And Jeremy said it to me last night. It's not something I need anyone to say. I didn't ask for this to happen, and though it occurred right under my nose, I didn't give consent. It's Chris's fault and his alone. But the picture the video paints is much different. So, whether or not it's actually my fault is irrelevant. Still, I smile up at Milly, grateful for her unwavering support.

A light knock gets our attention. Milly swings her gaze to the wall clock. "Looks like it's show time." She gives my shoulder a squeeze. "You okay to work today? If you need the day off, I can cover for you."

"Are you kidding? Not only am I ready, but I spent the better part of two hours cutting out hundreds of construction paper circles for the craft today." I flex my right hand, feigning a cramp from all the cutting.

She chuckles. "You did cut a lot! What are they for, exactly?"

I smile wide. Today is my favorite story time day.

"We're reading *The Very Hungry Caterpillar* for story time and we're going to make our own caterpillars to decorate the wall." I nearly squeal with excitement. That book has always been a favorite of mine and I love introducing it to young readers.

"You see, this is what I mean. You were meant for this library. You're a gift. Now, go on." She pats my arm. "Get ready for the bevy of tiny humans coming your way."

Strolling to the children's section, I feel lighter than I have in over a year, and I have Jeremy to thank for it. I never knew it was possible to feel this way about anyone, let alone a ghost. I'm not sure where we go from here, but I'm all in. And as soon as I get home, I'm going to tell him.

I plop my satchel onto the table and a few of the contents spill out. I scoop them up and begin placing them back in my bag when I discover a book that stops me. *What Really Happens When We Die: A Skeptics Perspective.*

I haven't looked through the book since the day Milly handed it to me. I want to say I've forgotten all about it, but I think it's more that I'm afraid. I originally requested it because I wanted to help Jeremy. He was trapped, and I wanted to free him. But now? Now I want to keep him forever, never letting him go. A few minutes ago, that felt romantic, but now it just feels wrong and selfish. How can I be with him while also letting him go? The answer is simple. I can't.

twenty-six

JEREMY

Darcy has been home for a little while. I couldn't wait to see her and rushed down to greet her the moment she walked through the door. Her behavior was strange. I'm not sure what I was expecting, but it wasn't what I saw. Her eyes were skittish, skirting around the room like she wasn't sure what to focus on. I asked her how things went with Milly and her answer was at odds with her face.

Milly was not only understanding, she was helpful. Thanks to her, Silas will no longer be a problem. That should delight Darcy, but there's no light in her eyes. Her skin looks sallow and her mouth is more frown than smile.

"Everything else okay?" I ask, hoping for some answer as to why she's acting like her entire world has collapsed.

"Mm-hmm. I'm just tired."

It might be the truth, though I know, for a fact, she slept soundly last night. I had my arms wrapped around her and she didn't so much as twitch the entire night. But I decide not to press her. She'll tell me when she's ready the same way she always does.

"Why don't you go relax on the sofa and I'll build a fire. It looks like it might storm."

She nods robotically and drifts into the living room. I cover her with a blanket the same way I did last night and get to work on the fire. She watches me with a hint of a smile playing on her face. "You know, when Mrs. Fitz first showed me this place, I figured I'd never use that fireplace. I don't know the first thing about building a fire. But thanks to you, I've …"

I wait for her to finish her thought, but she never does. Instead, she stands, striding out of the room. I finish what I'm doing, and once the fire is ablaze, I stand, walking in the same direction she did.

I find her in the kitchen, leaning against the wall, gazing out of the open sliding glass door. The sky has opened up and large drops of rain dot the deck boards. Darcy stares blankly out into the yard.

"Darcy? What's wrong?"

She laughs and it's laced with sadness. "What's wrong? What's right?"

I move closer, taking tentative steps like she may run off. "I don't understand."

Without another word, she steps out onto the deck, and when she spins around to face me, I can't tell if the moisture on her face is tears or raindrops. I join her, taking her face in my hands. "Tell me what's going on."

She looks up at the sky and then back at me. "You can't feel it, can you?" Her lip trembles and she steps back. My hands fall from her face. "I've been so selfish. So utterly self-consumed that I let it cloud my judgment. I wanted to help you, Jeremy. I wanted you to be free. Maybe you'll never be able to feel the rain on your face, but you shouldn't be trapped here like a prisoner."

"What are you saying?" My mind trips and falls as it tries to play catch up with her words.

"I'm saying I lost my way. I forgot my original plan because you are … well, you're you! And I wanted to keep you for myself. Even now, you're in there building a fire and I'm finding myself using it as yet another reason to hold you here."

"Hang on. You are *not* holding me anywhere. You and I? We are exactly where we're meant to be."

She shakes her head as I speak. "Stop. I'm here because I ran away from my problems. That's it. That's the big reason. And you? I don't know why you're here, but we need to figure it out so you can be free. Your soul deserves better."

I cross the deck until we're standing toe to toe. "My soul deserves you."

"Jeremy," she cries. "Look around! No one else can see or hear you. You can't feel anything. And when I'm not here, you're stuck in the attic. I don't know much about death, but that's no kind of life."

"Stop saying I can't feel things. I feel you." I wrap an arm around her waist, pulling her against me. "And you can feel me." I move closer until our mouths are inches apart. "I don't need to feel anything else in order to feel whole. You are every feeling, every sensation. You are at the center of my existence. For me, you are where everything starts and stops." I crash my lips to hers, capturing them in a fevered kiss. Our mouths move as one, and I taste the salt of her tears mixed with the sweetness that is uniquely her. How could she ever think I need or want anything more than what I hold in my arms?

* * *

DARCY

He steals my breath with his kiss, and I embrace it, hoping it somehow finds its way into his chest, filling his lungs. I will breathe for us both the same way my heart beats for the two of us. I still don't know if this is the right thing to do, but at this moment, I don't care.

How could anything that feels this right be wrong? Our mouths taste and explore as thunder cracks from somewhere behind us. The rain soaks our bodies, and even though I'm the only one who can feel it, I delight in the idea that I am all he can feel.

My hands raise and grip his suspenders, pulling him even closer. I feel him harden beneath his trousers and smile. Sensing my grin, he pulls back, eyeing me curiously. "What's that smile for?"

"You really *can* feel me, can't you?"

"You have no fucking idea." His mouth resumes its assault on mine as our tongues surrender to each other.

We kiss like it's the only thing we know how to do. Like we've found our destiny and we're chasing it together.

He breaks the kiss, rubbing a hand over his lips. His eyes turn feral as they roam over me, and I take a minute to appreciate the way the rain has made his shirt translucent. We stand still, bathing in the sight of each other. The heat in his eyes leaves a trail of warmth on my skin that begins at my breasts and travels all the way down my legs.

He reaches down, hooking an arm behind my knees. He scoops me up like I'm weightless. I lean forward at the same time he does, and for a brief moment, our foreheads press together, and we gaze into each other's eyes. And then his mouth fuses to mine and we devour each other. He moves us into the house, pulling the door closed with the toe of his shoe.

Our lips stay connected as he takes us into the living room. We pause our kiss as he lays me reverently onto the carpet in front of the fire. He stands above me, gazing down at me like a jeweler might look at a rare gem. "If I had any breath in me, you would take it away."

He kneels down beside me, brushing the back of his hand over my face. His fingers trail down my neck and move toward the buttons on my shirt. I lean into his touch as he unfastens each button. It feels like he's moving in slow motion, and I lift up my chest, encouraging him to hurry, but he shakes his head. "Do you know how long I've been waiting for this? I'd love to rip this shirt clean off of you, but you deserve to be savored."

I close my eyes, reveling in his touch as he peels my shirt open. His fingertips skate over the swell of my breasts, and the "barely there" feeling through my bra is enough to make me lose my mind. As if sensing my frustration, he reaches under my back and unclasps my bra. Leaning over, he sucks a nipple into his mouth while pinching the other with his fingers. It's sweet torture, and if he isn't careful, I might come undone from this alone.

He continues moving down my stomach, leaving a trail of kisses in his wake. When he reaches the waistband of my skirt, he lifts his face so that it hovers above the apex of my thighs. Slipping a finger under the elastic, he tugs my skirt off, taking my tights and panties along with it. I'm laid bare before him.

He stares at me, his eyes rabid with desire. Hooking his thumbs under his suspenders, he glides them off his shoulders and it just may be the hottest thing I've ever seen. Next comes his shirt, but he's less careful with his buttons and I appreciate the urgency. He stands, toeing off his shoes and shucking his pants and socks.

He reaches for the blanket on the sofa, taking it with him as he lowers himself over me. His forearms rest on either side of my head as he presses his lips to mine. This kiss is different than the one outside. It's soft and languid as he takes his time. It feels like being worshiped.

He kisses me until my lips feel puffy and bruised. His mouth moves down my body, placing kisses along the way. Taking a nipple in his mouth, he sucks hard before letting it pop from his lips. He does the same to the other and then continues down my stomach.

His mouth is warm, and I think I feel his breath on my thigh, even though I know it's impossible. He pushes my legs apart, kissing up and down them while carefully skirting over my most sensitive area. The place where I need him the most.

And then he's there, catching me off guard, pulling my clit into his mouth like a man possessed. He laps and sucks like I'm his last meal, only stopping when he senses I'm on the brink of losing control. "Don't come yet," he commands. I'm not used to him giving orders and taking charge, and nearly lose all sense of restraint. "Good girl," he rasps, and I have to close my eyes to stay focused.

He slows his pace, gently rolling his tongue over my clit with little to no pressure. I'm blinded by the torture, unable to see with my eyes rolling back into my head. "Please," I beg, feeling him chuckle as he presses a finger into me, making me cry out.

"Is that what you want? Hmm?"

"Yes," I moan.

"How about this?" he asks, adding another finger. I feel so full as he pumps his fingers in and out of me.

It's almost enough to take me to the edge. Almost. He senses my need for more and obliges, pulling my clit deep into his mouth. He's relentless as I writhe on the ground. "That's it, Darcy. Now let go." I ride his hand with unabashed fervor crashing over the edge. And the moment I do, a loud split of thunder booms from outside. He slows the movement of his hand and places a few soft kisses on my clit, sending shock waves of pleasure throughout my body.

When he's finished, he sits back on his heels, grinning down at me. He lifts his hand and sucks me from his fingers. "With you, I can feel *and* taste. And I fucking love it."

twenty-seven

JEREMY

I will never forget the way she looks right now, drunk with pleasure and completely sated. The soft glow of the fire bathes her in warm light, searing the image of her into my brain.

She sits up, meeting me halfway. Her lips press firmly against mine, and her tongue darts out, licking the seam of my mouth. I open for her and she enters and I will never get over how incredible this feels. Our mouths move like they're dancing to a song only we can hear.

She reaches between us and takes me in her hands, gasping at the fullness. "Not bad for a dead guy, huh?" I joke. She chuckles, lightly smacking me on the shoulder.

Looking down at my length in her hands, she licks her lips, and I bite back a moan. "I'd say it's a little more than just 'not bad.'" Her lips twist in an impish smirk, and then she lifts her hand to her mouth and licks from palm to fingertip. When she wraps it around me, I can no longer keep my eyes open. A deep moan escapes my lips. "You like that, huh?"

"Mmm," I hum.

"Then you'll love this," she says, lowering her head so that it's positioned between my legs. She takes my cock into her mouth, sucking deep. It feels like I must be probing the back of her throat, but she doesn't relent, continuing to bob her head up and down while cradling my balls in her hand. It's too much, and just before I explode, I put my hands on her shoulders, pushing her back.

With a mischievous grin, she rubs her fingers across her lips. "Sorry. I got a little carried away." She shrugs.

"You're not sorry," I tell her as I crawl over her, forcing her to lie back. "And neither am I." I kiss her with wild abandon, savoring every taste.

Me. Her. Us.

Positioning myself over top of her, I fist my cock in my hands, guiding it toward her entrance. But before I push inside, I lean my head back, gazing deep into her eyes.

"I love you. And I don't expect you to say it back. I just need you to know that this means everything to me. *You* mean everything to me. I love you, Darcy Simon." The words are like a crack in a wall wide enough for me to almost see through.

Her answer comes not with words but with tears in her eyes and an impassioned kiss. She kisses me like she's trying to breathe life into me, and I want to tell her she already has. Even though she hasn't told me she loves me. I already know. And it's enough. She's enough.

I push inside of her, and we both gasp. I stay still for a moment, letting the sensation linger. And when I start to move, her mouth parts, and she sighs my name. It spurs me on, and I pick up my pace, gliding in and out of her like I'm trying to permanently fuse our bodies. I chase the feeling that's building deep inside of me as Darcy screams my name. A streak of lightning fills the sky, bringing with it a flash of bright light. It illuminates her beautiful face glistening with sweat, her wild eyes on mine. And it's my undoing. I let out a guttural moan that ends with her name on my lips.

I try to hold myself up, but she shakes her head. "You told me before we touched that you felt the weight of things. I want to know what it's like to feel the weight of you. Don't hold back."

I squint at her. "Are you sure?"

"Absolutely."

I lower myself, fully sinking into her. She lets out a grunt, but when I try to lift up, she wraps her arms around my back, pulling me down against her. We stay that way for a few minutes, and then I roll off, positioning myself beside her. We keep our hands wrapped around each other like we're afraid if we let go, we may lose each other.

"You know, I think you may have been lying, Jeremy." There's a playful glint in her eye, but her words give me pause.

"About what exactly?"

"I don't think you're a ghost." She lifts up onto her forearm, sliding toward me until her face hovers above mine. "Dead guys shouldn't be able to fuck like that."

I laugh, and she catches it in her mouth, reminding me that even though I'm dead, I've never felt more alive.

* * *

DARCY

. . .

"No, no, for real. What do you think a cheeseburger tastes like?" I ask.

Jeremy keeps trying to convince me that he's perfectly content being a ghost, but I've been trying to get him to understand the importance of being able to taste certain foods. Namely cheeseburgers.

"I don't know." He shrugs. "Meaty?"

"Meaty? Are you for real? Next, you're going to say they also taste cheesy, right?"

He slaps a hand over his mouth, making us both laugh.

"I'm serious, Darcy. I don't care about any of that." His eyes flick back and forth between mine.

"I know you don't, but since I know what you're missing, it's hard for me to wrap my head around it."

"Oh, you know how to wrap your head around hard things, all right." He smirks as I gasp.

"Jeremy! Who knew you were so dirty in there?" I say, tapping a finger on his temple.

"I did," he says, grinning.

The storm outside has died down with a few lingering flashes of lightning here and there. We lie tangled beneath the blanket as the fire slowly dies out.

"Here," Jeremy says, sliding out from under the blanket. "Let me quickly throw some more wood on there."

"Do it fast. I need you under here to keep me warm."

He slides a finger along my forehead, sweeping a strand of hair from my face, and then he rushes off to stoke the fire. When he glides back underneath the blanket, I launch myself at him, climbing his body like a tree.

"You just can't keep your hands off me, can you?"

"I really can't," I say, burrowing into his chest. My feet feel like ice and it makes me wonder. "What do you feel when I'm wrapped around you like this?"

His lips press together. "It's hard to describe."

"Please try?"

He angles his head so he can look at me. "When I have you in my arms, it's a bit like remembering. There was a time when I didn't have to imagine texture. I just knew how it felt. Things like warmth and," he pauses, running a hand through my hair, "incredible softness weren't something I had to envision. But when I'm with you, holding you, touching you in any way, it feels like a memory. It stirs something inside of me. Something that says, 'Yes, this is how it feels. I remember now.'" He looks away. "That sounds insane, doesn't it?"

I press a finger to his chin, forcing him to turn his head and look back at me. "Not even a little bit."

He kisses the tip of my nose. "Don't ever stop being you, okay?"

I chuckle. "That's an easy thing to promise. If I'm not me, I don't know who I'd be."

The room is quiet, aside from the crackle of flames. There's a breeze outside that whistles as it blows around the house. I imagine it picking up speed and becoming a gale force wind. It lifts the house and sends it twirling through the air like we're Dorothy and Toto caught in a cyclone. Only when we land we don't crush any witches or frighten any munchkins. Instead, we find ourselves in our own secret world. A world where Jeremy is alive or I'm dead. It doesn't matter who ends up in what way as long as we're both in the same boat. I long to be dead with Jeremy or for him to be alive with me. And the longer we lie here, the more I begin to realize how unlikely that is.

"Hey," he whispers. "What are you thinking about? I can't read your mind, remember?" He gives me a crooked smile.

"Sometimes I wish you could." I sigh. "I was just thinking about what would happen if I died."

"What?" He sits up fast, knocking the blanket off of us. I grab the edge of it, tugging it back over me, but he stays upright, a frantic look in his eyes.

"I'm not planning on anything. It's nothing like that. I was just wishing there was a way to even the playing field."

"Even the playing field?" He speaks the words slowly as if he's hoping they'll take on a different meaning.

"Come on, don't tell me you haven't thought about it." I huff.

He rubs at the back of his neck. "About you dying? No, I definitely have *not* thought about that and neither should you. You're young. You have your whole life ahead of you."

"That's the problem."

"What are you saying?" he asks through clenched teeth, making me hesitate.

"I don't want to fight."

He shakes his head. "We're not fighting. I said you have your whole life ahead of you and you told me that was a problem. I just want to know what you mean by that."

"It's just ..." I bite might lip, refusing to cry. "Now that I have you, I don't want to lose you. And I don't know where we go from here."

His eyes soften and he slides down to rest on his forearm. "I feel the same way. I do, but you dying is never an option. Okay?" His eyes lock with mine.

I nod. "Okay."

The mood has shifted from lighthearted to somber, and I hate myself for making it happen. It was never about me actually dying. I have no plan to make that happen. I just wanted to be real for a moment. What we have is amazing, but it's not sustainable. Not like this.

For now, though, I'm not going to wallow. Because we have each other, and if it's only temporary, then we need to make it the very best temporary we can.

I lunge at him, catching him off guard, but he recovers quickly, wrapping his hands around my waist. I straddle him, shoving his shoulders flush with the carpet. His eyebrow quirks, but he doesn't say a word. I lean down close so that my mouth is nearly touching his.

"You had your turn. Now I have mine," I whisper.

He lifts his head, trying to kiss me, but I back away. "Ah ah ah," I scold. "I make the rules this time."

I sit up and find him hard and ready. "Good boy," I croon. "Now, here's what's gonna happen," I murmur. "I'm going to stick your cock inside me and ride it for as long as I want. Okay?"

His eyes flare with need and he nods.

I lift up and drop down fast, pushing him inside me. Both of us gasp, and I close my eyes as I clench around him. Then I do it again, slower this time. Lifting up and easing down. I don't pick up my pace, keeping it slow and even. This is going to last. My movements are agonizingly slow for both of us, and I can tell by the way he bucks his hips that he'd like me to speed up, but I won't oblige. Not until I'm good and ready.

"Please," he moans, and something about the word from his lips incites a primal urge inside of me. I increase my tempo and he meets me at every turn. As I drop down, he lifts up. We continue the give and take for a few more thrusts before I throw my head back, screaming his name as he whispers mine.

twenty-eight

DARCY

It's been three weeks. Three amazing, incredible weeks. I wake up every morning wrapped in Jeremy and fall asleep every night calling his name. And as for the moments we aren't in bed, though they are few, we spend the time nestled together reading and talking. We even started a book club. This week, we're reading *The Simple Wild* by K.A. Tucker. It's making me want to grab Jeremy and jet off on our own Alaskan adventure. I have to quell those thoughts when they start because nothing useful or good can come of them.

We still haven't figured out how to make this work in the long run, but I've been talking to him about buying the house from Mrs. Fitz's daughter. He thinks I'm joking, but she's been living in Hawaii for over a year and it sure doesn't sound like she has plans to return any time soon. Why would she still need the place? I haven't told Jeremy this yet, but I plan on talking to Mrs. Fitz about my idea when I drop off my rent check later today.

The library is quiet this time of year. Thanksgiving is next week and a lot of people are planning trips out of town to visit family. Speaking of family, my mom wasn't too thrilled to hear I won't be joining them this year. "This isn't still about that video, is it, Darcy?" My mom asked when I told her.

No, it's actually about a ghost whom I happen to love, though I still haven't said those words. I know he told me I didn't have to, but I will. I can't explain it, but I know there's a right time. A time when they'll have the greatest impact. So, I'm waiting for then. Or maybe I'll just tell him tonight while he watches me make dinner.

"Hey, you," Milly calls out as she rushes toward me. Her daughter arrives tonight and she's been jittery all day.

"Hey, yourself." I smile. "Has Amy's plane taken off yet?"

She swings her head around to look at the wall clock. "It should be in the air by now. She sent me a text from the airport. Said she was glad she decided to come up earlier to beat the crowd."

"I'm anxious to meet her."

"Oh, Darcy, you're going to love her and she is just going to be wild about you! I've told her all about you and she says she can't wait to meet the woman who gets to listen to me 'squawk' all day," she says, punctuating the word with air quotes.

I laugh. "It's not a hardship. I enjoy your company. In fact, I feel really fortunate to work here and to know you."

She makes a funny face and cocks her head. "You're not thinking of leaving, are ya? Because that sounds a little like you're gearing up to say goodbye."

I shake my head. "No, actually, I'm thinking of making myself more of a permanent fixture around here."

"Ooh! I like the sound of that!"

"Me, too." I grin.

This situation is far from ideal, but if my lemons are falling in love with a ghost, then my lemonade is buying the house he's currently haunting.

The rest of my day passes by in a flurry of toddlers and glue sticks. By the end of the day, I've scrubbed nearly every surface of the children's area. I'm in the staff lounge washing my hands when Milly walks in. "Whew, remind me to avoid any crafts that involve gluing when working with two-year-olds."

She wrinkles her nose. "Yeah, that's a ripe age for a sticky mess."

"It sure is! Well," I say, drying my hands off on a paper towel, "I'm off. Have a great time with Amy tonight. I look forward to meeting her soon!"

She smiles kindly. "Thank you! Now go on home and draw yourself a nice hot bath just in case there's any residual stickiness left anywhere."

I nearly snort but manage to contain myself. There will be stickiness all right and also a bath, but maybe not in that order.

Shoving the glass doors open, I welcome the crisp fall air. Most of the leaves are gone now and the ones that still hang on are brown and crunchy. I practically skip to my car but stop halfway when I see someone standing a few feet away.

"Silas," I stammer. "What are you doing here?" I glance behind me, but Milly must still be in the staff lounge.

Silas holds up his hands. "Don't freak out. I promise I'm

not going to do anything. And if it means anything at all, I hate myself for making you think I would."

I narrow my eyes at him, not trusting a word that comes out of his mouth.

He shoves his hands in his pockets and casts his eyes to the ground near my feet. "For what it's worth, I'm sorry. I never should've said anything that day. I've replayed it over and over in my mind, and I still can't believe any of it came out of my mouth."

"I haven't replayed it at all. In fact, I've barely given it any thought."

"Really," he says with a hopeful lilt.

I hold up a finger. "Not for the reason you think. I've wasted too much time worrying about everyone else's perception of me and people like you and my ex-boyfriend aren't worth my time. You feast on people when their self-confidence is at an all-time low and then you spit them out. You lack empathy and basic human decency. It makes me sad. Because chances are, you'll never get to experience what life has to offer. It will always elude you because you'll be too busy searching for the next Miss Right Now. And don't think for a second, I don't know why you're out here fumbling through an apology. It's only because you got caught. Now, if you'll excuse me." I walk briskly to my car, never giving him a second look.

I feel weightless as I pull out onto the road. What I just said to Silas is what I should've said to Chris once I'd discovered what he'd done. Instead, I begged for answers he never gave. I never confronted him or held him accountable for his actions. I just ran away. And after what happened with Silas, I thought I was going to have to run again.

Until Jeremy convinced me otherwise. He saw a

strength in me I'd long left for dead and he coaxed it out of hiding.

And now, me and my confidence are heading straight to Mrs. Fitz to ask the most important question I've ever asked.

* * *

JEREMY

There are certain advantages to being dead. Things I hadn't considered when I was pining for human attention.

I don't sleep. It was lonely at first, but now that I spend my nights lying next to Darcy, it's one of my favorite perks. Her eyes dance beneath their lids, and I imagine she's living a whole other life in her dreams. I long to join her in them.

I also have no use for eating, but Darcy does, and it's become commonplace for me to join her in the kitchen every evening as she prepares a dinner for herself. I've been watching closely and I've picked up a few things. There's a shelf of cookbooks up here and I've spent the day perusing them in search of the perfect recipe. Tonight, I'm trying my hand at cooking for her. It might be a disaster, but I want to do something for her, and my options are limited.

I make a plan to set up a picnic for us in front of the fire. A wicked grin curls my face as my thoughts take me back to that night. I may not have been able to feel the warmth of the flames, but the heat I *did* feel was all-consuming.

Flipping the iPad cover open, I glance at the clock. She should've been home by now, but maybe she got held up. It wouldn't be the first time. I smile, thinking about how lucky the library patrons are to have her around, getting the chance to interact with her in her element. I'd give anything for five minutes with her outside of this house where we feel like a secret.

I keep my eyes glued to the clock, and my ears tuned in, awaiting the telltale creak of the front door. The anticipation tricks me into feeling like I'm alive, but at the same time, I also feel half full, like I'm just a man playing dress-up, pretending to be human. It's times like this when I come face-to-face with the reality that this will not last. And I don't know what to do with that.

Finding Darcy has been like stepping into the sun after years of only night. I can't imagine retreating back to the lonely darkness after experiencing all of this, and yet, I don't see any way around it.

Darcy is alive and she's young. She should be out there living her life, not stuck in here chained to a dead man. We live in secret. No one can know because no one can see. She'd be dismissed as a crazy person if she ever told anyone about me. And I can't leave this house, which means if she wants to spend time with me, then neither can she. Together, we may be able to leave the tiny attic library, but we're still trapped. Nothing has changed.

Mostly, I shove these thoughts out of the way and it's easy when Darcy is here with me. I delude myself into pretending that we're married and enjoy spending our nights in. And it almost works. But there have been a few times when she's made mention of a place she'd love to visit or something she'd like to do, and I watch helplessly as her face falls the minute the realization hits her. She always shakes it off, pretending like it never happened, but I see it, and I feel it.

We have an expiration date. We've had it since the moment we met, and there's nothing I can do to change it, but what I can do is enjoy every second I have with her, soaking it up for a time when I'll need it most.

The front door opens and I'm up, launching myself like a rocket out of the room. I sprint down the stairs and into the foyer, calling out, "Wait till you see the surprise I—" My words freeze in my throat. Her face is red and mottled and thick streams of tears fall from her eyes.

Rushing toward her, I place my hands on either side of her face. My eyes flick back and forth between hers. She hiccups and coughs as sobs wrack her body. "Darcy? What happened?"

She swipes away tears and tries to find some composure. It's when she looks up at me that I know. I don't need her to say the words.

Our time is up.

twenty-nine

DARCY

"I was plannin' to come and see you in the morning," Mrs. Fitz said as she took hold of her hip with a meaty palm. "Karen finally left that good-for-nothin' Ralph and she's comin' home."

I squinted at her as though it might make her words clearer. "Home?" I echoed.

"Mm-hmm." She nodded. "But don't worry. No one's kicking you out on your behind just yet. She won't be back for another month. Said she was gonna do a little traveling on her way back. Stopping off here and there to see some sights, whatever that means."

The temperature outside was mild, but I felt so cold, I was sure I could see my breath. "Wait. She's moving back in there?" I jerked my thumb behind me toward the tiny little oasis I shared with Jeremy.

Mrs. Fitz huffed like she was growing tired of this conversation and I couldn't have agreed more. "Well, yeah. It's her house, after all."

My jaw was unhinged, and I couldn't find my voice. The corners of Mrs. Fitz's eyes softened, and she leaned in, patting my arm as she spoke. "Now, now, don't you worry. I've already spoken to Carla McKeal and she said you can rent the little bungalow on her property. It's only a few miles from here and it's even a little closer to your library."

I didn't care about any of that. I could easily find somewhere else to live, but no matter where I went, Jeremy would have to stay behind. And that thought paralyzed me. How had things derailed so quickly? I had come over here intent on offering to buy Karen's house, and within the span of a few minutes, I learned that not only was that not an option, but neither was continuing to rent it. It was just ... over.

The story pours out of me in one long stream as I sit on the floor in the foyer with my legs flopped in front of me. Jeremy remained quiet the entire time, and now that I've finished, he still hasn't spoken. He's likely just as shell-shocked as I was. As I still am.

"Say something, please," I beg.

His grip on my hands tightens as his eyes track the tears on my cheeks until they finally meet my gaze. We stare hopelessly at each other as though we're trying to pull a plan from somewhere deep inside. But none exists. I've had a few more minutes to digest this information, but it wouldn't matter if I had hours or even weeks. The fact remains that Jeremy cannot leave this house, and in a few short weeks, I can't stay.

"Maybe I can talk to Mrs. Fitz. Karen will probably need money if she's on her own. I could buy this house. It could work. I'll offer her double what it's worth. I have some savings and I'm sure I could get a loan—"

Jeremy's finger rests on my lips, silencing my rambling. "No matter how hard we tried not to think about it, you and I were always temporary. A once-in-a-lifetime chance encounter that will forever leave us changed. But it can't last. I don't think it was ever supposed to." He removes his finger, placing his palms on my cheeks.

He's talking as though he's following some unspoken guide and his words infuriate me, igniting my anger like he's trying to put out a fire with alcohol. I shove his hands away and push up to standing. "How can you say that? All nonchalant like this isn't affecting you?"

His eyes blaze, and suddenly he's standing, too. "I never said I wasn't affected. If I weren't already dead, I'd be certain I was dying now. I can't even begin to think about what my existence will be like once you're gone. But I don't want to waste a single moment of our time together dwelling on the things we can't change." He stalks toward me until we're standing toe to toe. Despite my dueling emotions, I shiver from his proximity.

His hands skate up the length of my arms and rest on my shoulders. Our foreheads pull together the way they always do in that familiar way I've never been able to explain. "I don't think I can handle this, Jeremy," I whisper.

"I know, but for now, you don't have to worry about any of it. Even though we have a date looming in the distance, it's far enough away that we can continue to exist in our bubble a little while longer." His voice is gruff and full of emotion. Our pupils dance an agonizingly slow waltz as we both process this information in our own ways.

Jeremy would rather put off thinking about it because he has already accepted defeat, but I'm not there yet. And I don't think I ever will be. There's a fix for this. I just have to figure out what it is.

* * *

JEREMY

Darcy's silence speaks louder than any words she might say. This news, though inevitable, has broken her. It's threatening to break us, but I won't let it.

She's terrified of losing me, but I don't see it in that way. I exist in a space where memories have failed me. I have inklings. Tiny morsels of who I might've been. Hints that appear to me as clues rather than actual recollections. But now, all of that has changed. Darcy has given me experiences that are invaluable. She has allowed me to cast aside the mystery of who I was and focus on who I am. And for that, I will never lose her. Even if she's gone from my present, she'll never be far because I will continue replaying my time with her on a loop for as long as I'm in existence.

I wrap my arms around her, and for a moment, she just lets me while hers dangle at her sides. And then I close my eyes as I feel her hands snake around my middle and clasp behind my back. The comfort her touch brings me is something I'll never be able to put into words.

"You know," I mutter against her hair, "I had big plans for tonight."

"You did?" she croaks.

"Mm-hmm. I was going to make you dinner."

"Oh, Jeremy." She starts to pull away, but I tighten my grip. "I don't think I can eat anything tonight. My appetite is long gone."

"You say that now, but I have a feeling you'll be singing a different tune once you taste my ravioli Alfredo." I pull back slightly, grinning at her.

She arches a brow and I can tell it's difficult for her to be playful with me, but I love her for trying. "Is that so?"

"Only one way to find out," I say, tipping my head toward the kitchen.

She chuckles and then stops abruptly, catching herself. This will take work, but I'm determined not to let her drown in despair. Taking her hand in mine, I lead her away from the door and away from the problems plaguing us. We can't escape them, but we can table them until they're unavoidable.

* * *

"Holy shit, Jeremy. Who knew you had a hidden talent for cooking?" Darcy groans over a mouthful of cheese filled ravioli—her second helping, I might add.

I snicker. "I'm not sure it's as much of a talent for cooking as it is for following directions, but nonetheless, I'll take the compliment."

The smiles and quips are coming easier now, though it was a bit of a struggle to get here. Darcy tried a few times to bring up Karen's impending move back home, but I thwarted the conversation at every turn. Eventually, she gave up, I think, because she realized I wasn't going to allow it.

I stoke the logs on the fire and watch as the embers spit in protest. The picnic was a brilliant idea, if I do say so myself. It's hard to feel down when you're cozy in front of a fire filling your belly with food. I don't have to be alive to realize that. And for me, just being in her presence is enough. I would say I'm soaking it in more now, but I've always done that. If there was a way to bottle up this feeling, I'd be the richest ghost on the planet.

"Oh! I forgot to tell you, I had another run in with Silas today," she says in between bites.

My hand cinches the blanket in a death grip. "What happened?" The words are a growl. I've never liked Silas, but after what he tried to pull a little while back, I despise him. I can't even let myself think about how he attempted to proposition her. For the most part, I've felt resigned to this existence, but when that happened, the desperation to leave this house and beat him to a pulp was nearly overwhelming.

"You would've been proud of me, actually." She winks. "He attempted to apologize, but I didn't accept. In fact, I pretty much crammed it back down his throat. Figuratively, of course." She shrugs, looking adorable.

I smile and let out a soft chuckle. "That's my girl."

Her face falls and her chin quivers.

"Hey," I croon, sliding over beside her. "What's wrong?"

"You don't need to ask, do you?" She lifts her head and her eyes swim with tears.

"No." I sigh. "I guess I don't."

"I'm just ... really going to miss us." She exhales the words like she's afraid to let them go.

"Me too."

I take the empty plate from her hands and discard it onto the coffee table. She stands and we begin to move in an unspoken rhythm. Our bodies dance around each other as we clean up dinner and extinguish the fire.

We climb the stairs in single file, with her leading the way. She drifts into her room and plucks her pajamas from her dresser, taking them to the bathroom with her. Moments later, she ambles back into the room to find me turning down the bed. She climbs in first, rolling to rest on her side with a hand tucked under her pillow. I lie beside her, curving my body around hers, silently marveling at the way we fit.

Minutes pass, and her breathing seems to even out. I hope she can find the peace in slumber that she can't seem to find when she's awake. And I wish more than anything that I could fix this.

I lean in close, placing a kiss behind her left shoulder, and she stirs, spinning around to face me. We hold each other's gaze captive, letting the moment build between us like a cup filling with water.

And then we overflow.

Our hands move quickly, covering each other's bodies like we're trying to memorize every crevice. Our mouths press together in the only way we can fathom communicating.

I lift the hem of her shirt and slide it over her head. She grips my suspenders and peels them off of me. My shirt is gone next, followed by her shorts, and in a span of seconds, we are stripped bare.

Skin presses skin and the friction intensifies. We're still facing each other as I push inside of her, making her gasp. I stay still, closing my eyes as I commit the feeling to memory. Nothing will ever compare to this.

I've read thousands of books with every type of romance imaginable, and I can say, without a doubt, that no love story will ever come close to the one we've written.

thirty

DARCY

I started packing three nights ago once I realized the deadline was looming close. I haven't gotten very far. I fold a shirt here and there or sort through a few pieces of jewelry, and then I have to walk away.

Carla dropped off the keys to her bungalow this afternoon. She was surprised I didn't want to see it before moving in, but it doesn't matter what it looks like. It could be a seven-bedroom mansion or a tiny closet for all I care. For me, home is where Jeremy is and Jeremy is here. So, unless I can stay in this house, I'll never be home again.

I've tried to compartmentalize these thoughts. I'm aware if I said them out loud, they'd sound dramatic, but that doesn't make them any less real. Jeremy has done his best to distract me and keep me in the moment, but the darkness has never been far. I've slipped into it when he isn't paying attention. At night, when he thinks I'm asleep, my mind swims with thoughts, some more dark than others. I want to stay with him, but I don't want to die, and I can't bring him back to life. So we're stuck.

And it sucks.

To make matters worse, he's been leaving me alone sometimes, retreating to the attic to give me the space he seems to think I need. And maybe he's right. Because when he's with me, all I can think about is how he's going to be ripped away. But when he's not here, I'm left with a desperate ache to be with him.

I've even started fantasizing about becoming best friends with Karen Fitz. Who knows, maybe she'd like a roommate? And then what? I move back in here and meet up with my ghost boyfriend in secret?

I shake my head at myself. I think I'm starting to lose it.

Jeremy clears his throat, and I look up to find him leaning against the doorframe. His lean yet muscular arms plunge into his pockets. He has an effortless beauty that leaves me breathless at times.

"Need some help?" he asks, jutting his chin toward my nearly empty suitcase.

"Sure. Know any good hitmen who need practice? If I were dead, I would never have to leave, and then all of this packing could be someone else's problem." My lips quirk into a crooked smile, but Jeremy's stay pressed tightly in a firm line.

He strides into the room and stops directly in front of me. His eyes hold mine captive in a fierce stare. "Is that supposed to be a joke? If it is, it's not funny. And if it isn't ..." He pauses, shaking his head and looking distressed. "Darcy, you can't use death to lighten the mood. I can't bear the thought of you no longer existing in this world."

"Yeah, but if I didn't exist in *this* world," I say with a

sweep of my arm, "then I'd exist in yours. Wouldn't that be the best possible outcome?"

I barely get the words out before he's vehemently shaking his head. "No. It most definitely would not. How can you even say something like that?"

I stand, keeping our eyes locked. He's several inches taller than I am, but I match the intensity of his gaze with my own. "How can you not? Don't you want us to be together?"

He raises his arms and lets them drop to his sides with a smack. "Of course, I do, but not like that. I don't want to trade your life for whatever the hell this is that I have. And there's no guarantee it would even work that way. Suppose you did die and instead of being here with me, you ended up haunting the storage room of a grocery store or the basement of an old hotel. You'd be dead and so would I, but we'd still be apart. There are no guarantees, both in life and in death. All we have is the here and now. And right here, right now, we're still together. So let's just *be* together. Because in the end, no one can take these moments and these feelings away from us. They will continue to exist even if we don't."

I let out a long, slow sigh. He's right, and yet I still can't bring myself to accept it. "It feels like we're giving up," I whisper.

He brushes his hand along the side of my face, tucking my hair behind my ear. "We're not giving up. We're giving *in*."

He leans down as I lift up onto my toes. We meet in the middle, our lips pressing together as our bodies hum with everything we can't put into words. And as much as I want to figure out a solution to our problem, when we're together like this, nothing else exists.

What problem?

* * *

JEREMY

Her breathing is quiet and even. I know she's been pretending often lately, but I'm fairly certain she's asleep now. Still, just to prove it to myself, I wrap my arms tighter around her, nearly wringing her body as though I'm trying to siphon some of her life for myself. If only that were possible. We already feel like two halves; sharing a heart and lungs doesn't feel like much of a stretch.

She lets out a small contented sigh. I lift up onto my elbow and watch her eyes sway beneath their lids. Tonight, they're slow and rhythmic. I hope that means she's found some peace in her dreams. Since we learned about her impending move, when she does sleep, her eyelids flutter in erratic spasms, and her body jerks and twitches all night.

Powerless is commonplace for me. I've not been in control of my existence—if that's what you want to call this —since I materialized in the attic. But Darcy gave me back some of my control. For a little while, I felt almost human. Now that's all changed. I've never felt less in control.

Her body stirs in my arms, and she turns, facing me. Her eyes stay closed, but her lips curve slightly. "Are you watching me sleep, creeper?"

I let out a gruff chuckle. "Of course. Would you expect anything less of your favorite stalker?"

"I'd be disappointed by anything less," she says, her voice brimming with amusement.

I trace the outline of her face with the pad of my finger,

starting along her forehead and slowly drawing down the side. When I reach her chin, I take it between my thumb and finger, tilting her face toward mine. My lips catch hers. Our mouths stay closed for a moment, pressing together like a prayer, or maybe it's more like a plea.

Life after death is clear. I wouldn't be here if it weren't. I haven't given much thought to the idea of an "all-knowing, all-seeing supreme being," but desperation has led me to making silent deals. Asking whoever is in charge to spare us. I may not have a heart beating inside my chest, but it doesn't mean I can't feel it breaking.

With our mouths fused, I beg for someone, anyone, to help us. Even though I don't expect an answer, I'm still disappointed when one doesn't come.

Darcy is the first to part her lips and mine follow. Our tongues collide, and our bodies move, and I wonder if maybe this is the answer. We can't change what's coming, but we can enjoy what we have while it's still ours.

My arms close around her, bringing her close. Her leg hooks around mine as her hands reach up to hold the sides of my face. I pull back just enough to look deep into her eyes and whisper against her mouth, "I love you."

She sucks in a breath and launches herself at me. I catch her, lifting her up to rest on top of me. Her hips rise, and in an instant, she crashes down onto me. We stay still for a moment, reveling in the feeling, and then she moves. Her body undulating as she moans.

As she starts to come apart, her lips tremble, and a bevy of words flow from her mouth in a shaky exhale, "I don't want to let go, Jeremy. I can't do it."

I sit up and grip her waist as she bucks and sways. "You never have to let go, Darcy." I thrust my hips and catch her gasp in my mouth. I kiss her like I need it to survive. Like she is the reason for my existence. The thought hits me like an explosion in my head. I continue my movements in quick succession as we reach our peak together. We crest the summit and free fall. Our bodies quiver and pulse as our eyes stay locked; silent professions of love pass between us.

As we come down from our high, I can't shake the idea that I might be right. Maybe Darcy is the only reason I'm here, and when she's gone, I will be, too.

"Hey," she murmurs as she runs her fingers through my hair. "Where'd you go?"

I find a smile for her, keeping my thoughts from breaking through. I'll never say them aloud. If she thought, for even a second, that I'd be gone once she left this house, she'd drive herself crazy trying to figure out a way to stay or worse ... join me. "My love," I say with a grin, "if I weren't already dead, I'd say I think I died and this is heaven."

"What if it is?" she asks, a hint of a smile playing on her lips.

"What if," I say, leaning in to kiss her.

She sighs into my mouth, letting her body relax against mine. When she pulls back, she nibbles my bottom lip. Her face scrunches as though she's trying to suppress a laugh.

I arch my brow. "Something funny?"

An adorable giggle escapes her mouth. "Just thinking about the grocery store storage room I may be haunting one day. All those shelves and boxes? It sounds amazing."

I reach down and pinch her side, eliciting a sharp laugh. Her body jerks against mine, reminding me we're still connected. I twitch inside of her and now it's her turn to raise a brow. "Are all ghosts this insatiable?"

I tip my head. "Probably. What else do we have to focus on, you know?" I shrug.

She grips my hair in her hands, pulling me down until

my face hovers inches above hers. "Lucky me." She breathes before fusing her mouth to mine.

Our bodies writhe as one, and for a moment, it feels like I'm breathing as I lose myself in her once again. If this is it for me, I've made peace in knowing I've experienced the best of life.

The best of death.

thirty-one

DARCY

How do I do this? How do I leave?

I've accumulated a little more since first moving in, and the bag at my side is the last of my things. I've been standing here in the foyer for at least thirty minutes, unable to move. Once I put this suitcase in my car, that's it. I'll be officially moved out.

Jeremy is in the attic waiting for me to come say good-bye. If it's this hard to put a bag of clothing in my car, how will I ever find the strength to see him knowing it's the last time?

I glance at my watch. Twelve eighteen. Karen will be here at one. Our time together has been reduced to minutes.

The thought sickens me but also propels me to push through the door and out to my car. I toss the suitcase into the trunk and walk briskly back inside, never stopping until I'm in front of the attic door. I don't know how to leave him, but if all we have has dwindled down to forty minutes, I'll need every second.

A moment later, I'm in the attic. My eyes scan the room and find Jeremy seated on the recliner. His body bends at the waist and his arms rest on bent knees. His gaze is fixed on the floor, but once he senses me, his eyes snap to mine. Butterflies swarm in my gut, and my arms tingle at my sides. My legs move on their own, rushing me toward him.

I lower to my knees before him, resting my hands on top of his. Bowing my head, I take in several quick breaths, trying to steady my chest and quiet my thoughts. Every second counts. It always has with Jeremy. Somehow, I think I've always known this moment would come, though I tried everything within my power to stop it.

"All packed, are you?" His voice rumbles with a deepness I feel in my toes.

My head bobs in answer, but my words are frozen in my throat.

His hands move under mine as he wiggles them free. He places them on the sides of my face, lifting my head up until I can't help but look directly at him.

It hurts and heals at the same time.

"Hi," he croons.

"Hi," I whisper back. I try my best to stay strong, but I can feel my resolve begin to crack. A lone tear tracks down my cheek, but Jeremy catches it before it falls.

He lifts his hand, pressing the wetness between his thumb and forefinger. "I'm keeping this."

"You should," I whimper. "It's for you."

"You should know, you're my favorite part of death," he says with a sad smile playing on his lips.

"And you're my favorite part of life," I murmur.

He brushes a stray hair off of my forehead and marvels at my face like I'm a rare panting.

I suck in a shaky breath. "I'm never going to be able to leave you, Jeremy."

"Shh, you're not leaving me. Sure, maybe you won't be here in this house, but for me, you'll never be gone. When all I thought I had was a bunch of mismatched chapters, you came along and filled in the blanks. You're my epilogue, Darcy." He presses his lips to my forehead.

"How?" I whisper. "An epilogue is where we get our happily ever after. But we've been robbed of that."

He pulls back, locking my eyes with his. "Don't you see? These past few months with you have given me more than every book on every shelf. The memories we've made have given me the best kind of happily ever after. One that will play on an endless loop in my mind until the end of time."

I tilt my head back and gaze at the ceiling. "When you say things like that, it only makes this hurt more."

He lowers to the floor in front of me, taking my hands in his. My eyes slowly find his and I nearly gasp at the love I see in them. "It wouldn't hurt if it wasn't real," he hums.

His arms cocoon around me, and I allow myself to fall into him. Minutes turn to seconds, and I know it's time to leave, but I can't make myself move.

Jeremy moves first, sliding his hands around to grip my shoulders. "It's time."

I blink through tears, hoping that somehow, I'll wake up from this nightmare. But when I open my eyes, I'm still here, and this is still goodbye.

We walk in silence toward the front door, knowing that once I leave, he'll be banished once again to the attic.

When we reach the foyer, I look up at him. "I don't

understand how any of this is fair. To give us all of this only to snatch it away? It's cruel."

His hand cups my chin. "What if it's not?"

My brow furrows, but before I can say anything, he continues. "You're focused on the losing part of things, but Darcy, look at what we've gained. There are people who go through life, and maybe even death, never experiencing even a scrap of what we have. *That* is cruel."

"You know, for a dead guy, you're awfully insightful." I give him a sad smile.

"I've had a good teacher," he says, tapping me on the nose.

My watch buzzes on my wrist. I set an alarm for twelve fifty-five. Time to leave.

I turn toward the door, but quickly swivel back. "I can't." I gasp.

He presses a finger on my chin, tilting my head. "You can."

With an arm around my waist, he guides me to the door. His hand grips mine, bringing it to the knob. Together we turn it, and with a soft click, it cracks open.

"This isn't goodbye, you know?" he says. "There are no goodbyes for true love. You will always be here." He points to his head.

I slip through the opening until I'm on the porch. The door is like a force field between us. I can feel the separation pulsate through my veins. I open my mouth to say the words I've held back. "Jeremy, I—" He reaches out, pressing a finger to my lips.

"I already know."

* * *

JEREMY

I know the moment she's in her car because I'm suddenly whisked back to the attic. And it's there, alone with my thoughts, that I finally allow myself to accept the crippling realization.

She's gone.

For one brief moment, I had everything, and now it's over. And here I am, back in this attic where, in a lot of ways, I'm worse off than I ever was before. Because now I know what I'm missing.

I wonder if it's possible to will myself out of existence. I don't know where I came from or how long I'm supposed to be here, but haven't I been through enough? If I've had any debts, I've surely paid them. If there was a point to all of this, I'm ready for that to be revealed to me.

"I'm ready to leave now," I shout into the emptiness around me. "Do you hear me? I said, I want to go to … wherever that is. Just … anywhere, but here."

I pause, straining to hear a sound. Any sound at all. When nothing comes, I hobble toward the recliner and sag into it.

This is where I'll stay until whoever is in charge decides it's time for me to move on. I don't want to read anything else because I know nothing I find on these shelves will even so much as touch what I had with Darcy. There's nothing else for me here.

thirty-two

DARCY

I'm at the library on a Sunday, but over the past few weeks, it's become the norm. I practically live here now. My little cottage is cozy and cute and so very quiet. It's the kind of quiet that amplifies everything else. Every thought I have is in stereo. And if I'm left alone with my thoughts for too long, I feel like I'm suffocating.

Milly's here somewhere, though I haven't seen her much today. I'm pretty sure she suspects something is up with me, but I'm grateful she hasn't asked. So much has happened. I wouldn't even know where to begin. But these last three weeks have nearly broken me.

That first night at the cottage was absolute hell, but then I remembered the iPad I had given to Jeremy. For one brief moment, I felt a sense of relief knowing I could still communicate with him. It wasn't remotely comparable to actually being with him, but at least it wasn't goodbye.

I plucked my phone from my pocket and sent a quick

hello text. In an instant, all the happiness I was feeling disappeared when I heard the familiar chime of the iPad coming from one of my suitcases. At first, I thought maybe I was hearing things. I hoped that was the case. But then I tried to FaceTime Jeremy, and within seconds, I found the iPad stashed among my clothes.

I didn't put it there.

Jeremy must've shoved it in there when I wasn't looking.

As I sat on the floor surrounded by the clothing I had tossed aside, I held onto the iPad, still ringing from my unanswered call. Rejection seeped deep into my bones. I knew we couldn't be together, but I still had hope that things would change. Sure, Jeremy had behaved as though things were more final, but I just thought he was trying to stay strong for me. Knowing he had the wherewithal to sneak the iPad into my bag had me questioning everything.

Weeks have gone by, and I've moved past the hurt. I spent a few days in the anger stage, but it didn't last long because it wasn't fair. I think I've finally reached accep-tance. I don't like it, but I don't need to.

What Jeremy and I had *was* real and magical, and it was never going to last. The playing field isn't level. It's not even in the same realm. By giving me back the iPad, he was only trying to protect himself and me.

Lately, I've been thinking about leaving Baker Hill. The thought sickens me, but the idea of staying in this town and living so close to the love of my life, knowing we can't be together, is devastation on a level I never knew I could feel. I haven't mentioned anything to Milly yet, but there's no time like the present.

I stand, brushing my hands along my pants, and meander through the stacks toward Milly's office. As I near the door, the hushed sound of murmured voices gives me pause. The library is closed, and I didn't hear anyone come in, but I was pretty lost in the sea of construction paper fish I was cutting out, so it's possible I just didn't notice. I consider walking away, but something compels me to keep moving.

Milly's at her desk, speaking to a woman seated in the chair across from her. I've never seen the woman before, but she's striking with long, wavy, gray hair that reaches her waist and a lavender flowing dress that looks hand-made. Her eyes find mine, and for a moment, I'm transfixed by their cerulean glow.

She rises to her feet with such grace, it's as if she's floating. Her hand extends toward me, taking mine before I even have a chance to offer it. A strange warmth settles over me, starting in my gut and spreading out to my extremities. She smiles knowingly as though we share a secret. "My now, it's so nice to finally meet you, Darcy. We're going to be fast friends; I just know it."

My brow furrows as I look from her to Milly. My boss regards my interaction with a wide grin and a pleased gleam in her eyes. When she sees me looking at her, she gives her head a slight shake as though she's waking from a dream. With a clap of her hands, she brings herself back to the present. "I'm sorry, Darcy. You must be wondering who this is." She chuckles, and I join in, though it's impossible to mask the nervous lilt in my laugh. The woman is still holding my hand hostage and hasn't taken her eyes off of me. It's unnerving.

Milly stands, gesturing toward the mystery woman as she says, "This is Luna. I don't know if you remember, but a while back you told me you were interested in the afterlife."

It doesn't take long for me to remember. It was the day

Milly delivered the book I had requested. She mentioned this woman—Luna—telling me she was "connected" to the spirit world. Huh. This should be interesting.

I nod, smiling. "Yes, I remember. It's very nice to meet you, Luna." I give the hand she's still holding a shake and Luna's face crinkles with her grin. She finally releases her grip, and I swear my skin tingles from my palm to my fingertips.

Luna turns to Milly. "Thank you for always allowing me to patronize the library during off hours. It's so much nicer without all the whispering."

Milly smiles. "Happy to help."

Luna's eyes are on me as she nudges her chin toward the open door. "Now, Miss Darcy, why don't you show me what you've done with the children's area. It's been quite some time since I've been here and Milly tells me you've made some incredible changes."

"Oh, I, uh," my voice catches in my throat. I try to clear it, but Luna just winks at me, and something passes between us. It feels soothing, like a balm. The next time I speak, my voice is calm and sure. "I'd love to show you. Please follow me."

We make our way over to my little corner of the library. Luna marvels at the bulletin board like she's looking at the Mona Lisa instead of a garden mural filled with pipe cleaner flowers. "It's incredible what you've done." She spins on her heel, letting her eyes dance over the space. "It feels very welcoming. The children must love you."

"I haven't had many complaints," I offer with a half shrug.

She floats through the area, stopping at the little round craft table. She plucks out a chair and takes a seat, gesturing toward the chair next to her. As soon as I sit, unease begins to creep up my arms, taking root in my shoulders. I fidget with my hands, clasping and unclasping them in my lap.

Luna remains quiet for an impossibly long time, keeping her gaze on me. "You know, some people go their whole lives never finding love and you've not only found it once, but twice. But you've also lost it twice as well."

Her words leave me stunned. I know Milly mentioned she had connections to the other side, but I'm stuck on the word "twice." Surely, she can't be referring to Chris. I didn't love him. I only thought I did. But once I met Jeremy, I knew I'd never experienced real love before.

I don't reply, but Luna doesn't seem to expect me to. She continues on, "I assume from the short conversation back there with Milly that you know about my gift." She lifts a brow and leans in, waiting.

"Um, Milly said you had connections to the spirit world." The words slip from my mouth and I wish I could scoop them back up and swallow them. I didn't mean to lay it out like that—so blatant.

But Luna seems unbothered. In fact, she looks rather pleased. She nods a few times. "Yes, I suppose that's one way to put it." She stands, drifting across the room to examine my cart of supplies. Probing the markers with her thumb, she says, "I see things. And I hear things. I'm not ashamed of it, but it tends to make people uncomfortable. Hence, why I come here during off hours. No one likes it when someone knows their secrets."

I swallow hard. Does that mean she knows about the video with Chris?

"I can't read thoughts, if that's what you're worried about." She glances up at me and must see the concern in my eyes because she quickly adds, "I read emotions. Actually, I can feel them. For instance, with you, I can feel the love and the loss, but there's something more. Something you haven't figured out for yourself yet. But you will."

My brow furrows. "I'm not so sure about that. If you can enlighten me at all, I'd be grateful," I say with a chuckle.

"Hmm, well, I can tell you that ghosts don't just appear without a reason. You already know that though, don't you?"

I find myself nodding almost immediately. Jeremy and I have both wondered why I could see and hear him when no one else could. And my presence made it possible for him to leave the attic. It didn't make much sense, but I knew we had to be connected in some way. But wait—

"How did you know there was a ghost? You said you can read emotions, but that's pretty specific."

She laughs. "You're right, I *did* say I can read emotions, but that's not all I can do." She taps a finger to her chin. "Let's see. How can I put this so that it makes sense?" Her eyes scan the room and catch on one of the bookshelves. She breezes toward it, scooping up a book. Holding it up, she says, "People are like books. I know, I know, how original, right?" She rolls her eyes, chuckling. "But it's more sophisticated than that. Some people—just like books—are more interesting than others. When I see someone, I get a sense of who they are … a synopsis, if you will. And if they're more open, I can choose to read on."

Drifting across the room, she stops in front of me, looking down at my face with an impish grin. "And you, my dear, are not only open. Your book's pages turn on their own." My face twists with confusion, and her smile widens. "You're connected, too, Darcy."

I start shaking my head subtly at first, but then more

emphatically. "No, I don't see or hear things like you do. I mean … I see and hear one person, but …"

She rests a comforting hand on my shoulder. "You see and hear *your* person. Have you ever wondered why that is? Why you're the only one who can interact with him?"

Letting go of all pretenses, I allow myself to launch into this conversation, accepting that she just *knows* things. I've been communicating and living with a ghost for months, so this isn't actually the strangest thing that's ever happened to me. "Of course, I've wondered that. Jeremy has, too. But we just figured we were meant to be in each other's lives or, um, well, you know what I mean."

She smiles. "I do. And you're right. You were definitely meant to be. You have the kind of love that transcends time. It's lasting. And if you think you've only just met, you are sorely mistaken."

My gaze casts down to the tweed carpet beneath my feet, catching on a small pull. I stare at the loop and let her words wash over me. *If you think you've only just met, you are sorely mistaken.* But we did only just meet, didn't we? During our time together, there were moments, glimpses of something, but none of the pieces ever quite fit together. Luna's words are a lot like this loose thread on the carpet. I reach down and take it between my fingers, tugging it until the entire fiber unwinds. It stands straight up, stretching toward the ceiling. I grab my scissors from the table and snip it off. Weaving it between my fingers, everything begins to make sense.

thirty-three

DARCY

Our little library archives only extend to back issues of the Baker Hill Press, which was started in the early nineties. Definitely not far enough for what I'm looking for.

Milly once mentioned the Studebaker Central Library had microfiche going back to the early nineteen hundreds. She brought it up when we were discussing the origins of the home I was renting, but I quickly dismissed it then since it would've been like trying to find a needle in a haystack. Instead, I opted to pay our small township building a visit to look at zoning maps, which is how I learned when the home was built and by whom.

It wasn't until Luna opened my eyes to the possibility that Jeremy and I had known each other before—something I inherently already knew to be true—that I was overwhelmed with the need to investigate it further. Truthfully, I think I was afraid more than anything. I didn't want to find out anything that might send Jeremy away. But now that we're not together, I have less to lose and more to gain. And that's when I remembered the microfiche. I immediately sprung from my seat. Any other person would've jumped at my quick action, but Luna wasn't "any other person." She only laughed and said, "Go on. You know what you need to do."

I hastily thanked her and left without even so much as a "see ya later" to Milly. I'll have to explain it away later, but for now, I'm laser focused.

Pulling into a parking space, my car jolts from the quick stop. I leap out of the door and dash across the asphalt. When I reach the glass double doors, it takes everything in me not to start pounding away like a crazy person. I make myself knock with a few short raps and wait. My body jitters and shakes with anticipation.

Jim Kowalcyk ambles toward the door like he's out for a Sunday stroll. I want to scream at him to hurry, but I'm lucky he's even here and willing to do a favor for a fellow librarian. I called him from my car just before I left to drive over and was overjoyed—though not surprised—to find that he had come in to file some paperwork. Librarians tend to enjoy working during the off hours when it's peaceful and quiet. Jim and I met at Book Fest. He's the head librarian here and is a jovial man, albeit relentlessly wordy.

"Darcy! So good to see you! Come on in." He props the door open with his elbow and ushers me inside.

"Thanks so much for doing this for me, Jim." I smile at him.

He grins, letting the door shut behind him. "I was here anyway. It's not a problem at all."

He leads me toward the microfilm machine, all the while regaling me with a story about a mishap when ordering new pens for library patrons. The pens were misprinted with Central Studebaker Library instead of Studebaker Central Library, and, oh, the chaos that ensued. After what feels like we must've taken the "scenic" route to get here, we reach the machine. It always amazes me that these things are still in existence.

"You'll find everything you need in here," Jim says, gesturing toward the wide cabinets filled with microfiche.

I nod in thanks, hoping he'll hustle off to another place in the library, but this is Jim we're talking about. And just as I suspected, he doesn't make a move to walk away. Instead, he places a hand on his hip and scratches at his temple with his other hand. "What'd you say you needed these for again?"

I didn't. I only asked to come use the machine and had foolishly hoped he'd leave it at that. I mentally chastise myself as I rush to create a reasonable excuse. "Well, I was thinking about introducing the kids to some local history, and uh, you know, our library archives are limited so ..." I drift off purposely. Lying doesn't come very naturally to me, and while my reason for being here has nothing to do with story time, I did, in fact, want to introduce a local history unit with the kids, so at least that part isn't a lie. I bite the inside of my lip, waiting for his response.

He nods deeply. "Mm-hmm, yes, that's a fine idea. Well, I'll leave you to it, then."

Wow! Is it really that easy?

Nope.

Jim gets only a few feet away before stopping and spinning back around. "Say, did I ever tell you about how I almost majored in history?"

Considering we only met once before, you'd think I wouldn't know much about him, but in the forty-five minutes we spent with each other, he never stopped talking. I learned his entire life story, including this very fact. I nod, "Uh-huh, I remember you telling me about that."

"Yeah, it's always been a bit of a hobby of mine. History, that is. I love artifacts and actually, that reminds me. I just visited Wellington this past weekend. You know there's this quaint little antique shop right off of—"

The phone in his office rings, and I say a tiny thank you to whatever gods helped make that happen.

"Sorry. I'd better go get that. To be continued!" He winks at me before rushing off.

I let out a small sigh as I tug open one of the large drawers. Hundreds of little annotated boxes are splayed out before me. Each one lists years followed by months. I think back to when I went looking for the origin of the house I'd been renting. I learned it was built in 1939, so I decide to start there, plucking out the first six months of the year.

Settling into a chair, I get to work cycling through the film. It's a tedious process, especially since I'm not even quite sure what I'm looking for. After an hour, I've only made it halfway through February. I could be here all day.

Luckily, Jim still has whoever was on the phone held hostage with a story about some fishing trip he once took. Bits and pieces of the one-sided conversation drift through the quiet library, providing a sort of strange soundtrack to my task.

More hours pass and I'm nearly through the stack of film. I load May into the machine and continue on. Twenty minutes later, I'm scrolling through articles when a headline catches my eye.

Young Couple Dies in Tragic Accident

My entire body erupts in goose bumps as I read on.

Aaron Jeremy Wentling, 26, of 1634 Everly Lane,

Baker Hill, and wife, Anne Darcy Wentling, 26, were killed in a head-on collision near Highway 1. The driver of the other vehicle has not been identified and is said to be in intensive care at Studebaker Hospital.

Those names.
That address.
All the air leaves my lungs, and my heart pounds like it wants out of my chest.

A small photo accompanies the article. The picture is grainy, but I'm able to zoom in, and when I do, there's no mistaking what I see. The hair on the woman is shorter, but even still, it's like looking into a mirror. And the face on her husband is one I'd recognize anywhere. It's the same face I saw hiding behind a bookshelf in the attic months ago. One I'd come to love more deeply than I ever thought possible.

With a shaky hand, I print out the article and the enlarged photo. I fold it carefully and shove it into the pocket of my jeans. Moving quickly, I return the film to its box and collect the others, stowing them back into their spot in the drawer.

I move through the stacks like I'm in a trance, stopping by Jim's office, grateful to find him still on the phone. I mouth a quick "thank you" and wave.

My drive back to Baker Hill is swift, and before I even realize it, I'm stopped along the side of the road. Glancing out my window, the familiar home sits to my left.

I'm reminded of that first day when I pulled up to this house and couldn't believe my luck. It feels like a lifetime ago, and yet even now, those same feelings overwhelm me. It's different but also the same.

I lift myself out of the car, shoving the door closed

behind me with a *thud*. As I make my way toward the path, I realize I have no plan. I only spoke to Karen for a few minutes on the phone when she called to thank me for taking such good care of her home, but we never actually met. And now here I am, showing up unannounced at her home.

"She's not there," a familiar voice calls from across the street. Mrs. Fitz stands on her porch like a censure with her hands on her hips. "She left two days ago. Back with that damn Ralph again," she grumbles with a shake of her head.

"Oh," I say. "Well, I, um, just thought—"

"Forget something?" Her question comes at the perfect time because, yes, I did forget something. And it's burning a hole in my pocket.

I nod, but before I can say anything more, she struts across the street. "I can let you in. Doubt she'll be back anytime soon."

We meet at the front door, and she pushes her key into the lock. Twisting the knob, the door opens with a *creak* and we both peer inside. It looks the same as it did when I left, and it's all I can do to hold myself back from dashing up the stairs to Jeremy.

She juts her chin toward the foyer. "Go on in. I'll be back in a little while to lock up."

I mutter a quiet *thank you* and breeze inside. Mrs. Fitz shuts the door, and in an instant, I'm running, taking the stairs two at a time. I reach the attic door at the end of the hallway, and suddenly I'm filled with paralyzing dread.

What if I'm too late?

What if he's already gone?

thirty-four

JEREMY

I feel her before I see her.

I've been sitting in this chair for so long. It could be days or weeks—I can't be sure. I thought once Darcy was gone, I'd be swept away. Turned into dust and blown off into ... well, I don't exactly know, but someplace other than this attic. After all, what else could there be left for me to do here?

But now, something shifts in the atmosphere. The air around me crackles.

She's here.

I rise from my seat, my body vibrating with anticipation.

Taking tentative steps, I glide toward the stairs. For a dead guy, my ears work incredibly well. Hearing is probably my strongest sense, and yet, even as I strain, I hear nothing.

Am I imagining this?

Maybe she isn't here at all.

Maybe this is the end. The final few seconds before I drift away into nothingness.

And then the door flings open and she's there. Breathless and beautiful. Her eyes lock on mine and hold steady as she seems to float up the steps, stopping inches from me.

"Are you real?" The words leave my mouth all on their own.

She nods as an easy smile slowly blooms on her face. And then she launches herself at me, throwing her arms around my neck as mine encircle her waist. I lift her up and she looks down at me. I lower her in tiny increments and our foreheads meet, skin kissing skin. "God, I missed you," she breathes.

I close my eyes, savoring her words. "I've missed you, too," I whisper.

We stay that way, held together in each other's arms, and I wonder, again, if this is the end. She feels real, but maybe this is a grand illusion, or maybe it's a gift. One last embrace before it all goes away.

My arms tighten around her just as hers begin to loosen, dropping away from my neck. She grips my shoulders, and a rush of words tumbles from her lips. "I don't know how much time we have, and there's so much I need to tell you." I reluctantly loosen my arms from her waist and she sucks in a breath before continuing. "So, I met this woman—Luna—she's connected in some way to the other side and she knew about you, Jeremy. She knew about *us*."

I cock my head. "Knew about us how, exactly?"

"That's just it; I don't really know. But she said you wouldn't be here without a reason and it got me thinking." She shakes her head. "No, that's not right. I've already been thinking, but I was suppressing those thoughts because I was afraid if I explored them, they'd lead me down the wrong path and I'd lose you. But now, what else is there to lose, right?" She lifts a shoulder in a half shrug. "Anyway, I went to the city library and used their microfilm machine to search through back issues of the newspaper. I chose 1939 since I knew that's when this house was built and I made it to May when I found this." Plunging a hand into her pocket, she pulls out folded pieces of paper and holds them out to me.

I take them from her, and she watches with earnest eyes as I carefully unfold them. It's an article about a couple who died. I scan the words, my eyes catching on the names. "Their middle names," I whisper. "They're the same as ours."

She nods. "They are and there's more. Look at the next page."

I do as she says and freeze when I see the faces staring back at me.

Our faces.

"It's us." I whip my head up and capture her eyes with mine. "I don't understand …"

She takes my hands in hers; the paper crinkles between my fingers. "It's a lot to take in. I'm about an hour ahead of you and my brain is still spinning, but Jeremy, we were married and this address," she tugs the papers from my hand and points to the article, "it's the address of this house. You built it. Aaron *Jeremy* Wentling. It's the same name I saw when I looked at the zoning maps all those months ago, but without the middle name, I didn't make the connection. That's why you're here. This is our home."

I lift my head to look at the ceiling as I let the dust settle from the bomb Darcy just dropped. How can this explain so much while still bringing up so many questions?

"I know it's overwhelming." She hums. "But actually, it

makes so much sense and I'm so mad at myself for not investigating this sooner." Her gaze drops to the floor and her hands fall limp at her side.

There's one question swirling in my head that's louder than the rest. "If we died, why aren't you on this side with me instead of being alive?"

"I, honestly, have no idea. I must've been reincarnated? God, I can't believe I'm even saying that, but what other explanation could there be?" She bites at her lip, looking pensive.

Cupping her chin in my hand, my eyes search hers. "So … what now?"

* * *

DARCY

He asks the question, but not in an expectant way because he knows I don't have the answer.

Or do I?

My feet begin to move on their own, taking me across the attic library. I stop at Jeremy's "clue" shelf and reach for the old leather-bound book. The one that's been hollowed out.

A small smile plays on my lips as I find the black box nestled inside. I feel him at my back as I pluck the jewelry box out of its hiding spot. I slide the book back onto the shelf and turn slowly, cracking the lid open to reveal the gold bands inside.

"These are ours," I say with no definitive proof. Just a strong feeling.

Plucking the rings from inside, I hand the thicker one to

him. It rests in his open palm, and he closes his hand around it, locking it inside his fist. We look at each other; a silent plan passes between us. I take the delicate gold ring in my hand and slide it onto the ring finger of my left hand, at the same time, Jeremy slides on his.

I don't know what we were expecting to happen. Maybe a flash of light or a jolt of electricity. Something.

But to our dismay, none of that occurs. We're exactly who we were moments ago, except we're wearing rings now.

I look up at him just as he looks at me and then it happens. Memories, warm and rich, begin to flood my insides like an uncorked dam.

Our wedding was on a Tuesday at sunset. It was small, with only our parents and a couple of friends in attendance. We had only known each other for a few months, but in those months, we lived a lifetime. Jeremy surprised me with vows he had written. "I will love you in this life and the next and the next."

I smile at him. "You kept your promise."

"You remember, too?" he asks, tucking a strand of hair behind my ear.

"I do." Closing my eyes, I let the memories wash over me.

"We couldn't afford rings," he says. "You told me it didn't matter, but it mattered to me. For months, I saved up money until I had enough. I had planned on surprising you that day. I wanted it to be special, so I hollowed out this book and hid the rings inside. I was going to bring you up here and give you clues until you found it. But we never made it home."

"Yes, we did." I smile as tears slide down my cheeks. "It just took a little longer, that's all."

I feel his lips on mine, and I welcome the intrusion. I

never thought a kiss could top the ones we shared over the past several months, but this one surpasses them all. Because it has the one thing the others lacked. Remembrance.

I pull back for a moment and press my hands against his cheeks. "I love you."

His eyes close as he savors my words, and when they open, he wastes no time. Lifting my chin, his mouth captures mine, and we pour everything into each other.

Our dreams.

Our love.

Our hope.

And I begin to wonder if maybe we've cracked the code somehow. Maybe by sliding on these rings, we've bridged the gap between our two existences.

But then reality bursts through the door in the form of Mrs. Fitz. The wood floor creaks beneath her feet as she waddles into the foyer, calling out, "Find what you were looking for?"

We break apart, and I feel physical pain. "No," I whisper. "It can't end like this?"

Jeremy grabs my hands and holds them between us. "Listen to me, we will *never* end. I found you once. I'll find you again." He presses a kiss to my forehead and then he backs away.

Glancing between him and the stairwell, I don't know how to make my feet move. But somehow, I do the impossible, and I walk away from him again.

My feet trudge a weary path down the first set of stairs and the next until I'm facing Mrs. Fitz. She must see the sadness in my eyes because hers flash with concern. "Honey, are you all right?" I don't even have a chance to reply before her attention is immediately directed at the stairs behind me. Her mouth rounds. "Oh, I didn't realize you had someone with you. Aren't you gonna introduce me to your friend?" Her hands rest on her hips and she arcs a brow.

I whip my head around to find Jeremy standing behind me, his face frozen with a stunned expression. "You can see him," I choke.

Her face scrunches. "Of course, I can see him!"

My mind is playing catch up, but I quickly try to recover. "Sure, I know, what I meant is, he was always here. You just didn't see him before."

She nods but still looks confused. "Yeah, I definitely haven't seen him before. What's his name?"

"Oh, sorry," I rush. "Mrs. Fitz, this is my ... um ... this is Jeremy." He rests a steadying hand on my shoulder, giving me a light squeeze. I look up at him with a smile so wide it hurts, and when I speak again, my voice cracks. "Jeremy, this is Mrs. Fitz."

Jeremy's smile rivals mine. His eyes stay glued to mine as he replies, "It's so nice to meet you, Mrs. Fitz."

Three months later

JEREMY

The air is crisp, and the sky is crystal blue. A light wind whispers softly through my hair. Milly stands with me under an arbor in the gardens of Studebaker Central Library. She's clutching a notebook against her chest as though she's hoping the words on the page will melt into her. Over these past few months, I've gotten to know her well, especially after she hired me to work the front desk at the library. It's been so good to not only work with books but to be around people.

"It's okay, Milly. I'm sure you'll be just fine," I assure her.

She shakes her head. "I hope so. It's just, this is kind of a big deal. Are you sure you trust me with this?"

I chuckle. "Well, it's a little late to change our minds now, isn't it?"

She winces. "Yes, I suppose you're right. I'm just feeling a little overwhelmed, is all. But don't you worry. It'll be perfect."

I smile. "I know it will. There's no other option."

She leans over, taking my bow tie in her hands. With a small tug, she grins. "There. Now it really is perfect."

A moment later, the haunting melody of "I Found" by Amber Run begins to play. All eyes drift down the flower laden aisle as we wait for my love to appear.

I steal a quick glance at Darcy's mom, seated in the front row. She smiles warmly at me. She wasn't an easy sell, especially after what her daughter had been through with Chris. But I won her over fast with my persistence in making Chris pay for what he did to Darcy. With Milly's help, I convinced Darcy to contact a lawyer. All it took was one strongly worded letter and Chris immediately removed the video from the website. I'm not ready to let him off the hook so easily, but for now, it's enough.

My eyes surf the rows of chairs filled with residents of this small town; all of whom love Darcy, which is no surprise to me. I find Luna a few rows behind Darcy's mom. She beams at me. Mrs. Fitz and her husband, Bill, sit beside her. Mrs. Fitz looks around at all the people in her judgy sort of way while Bill keeps looking at his watch.

My mind flits back to the day when everything changed. Once we realized Mrs. Fitz could see me, it was nearly impossible to contain our excitement. She blathered on about her daughter, Karen, for what felt like hours, and all the while, I was noticing so many things I hadn't at first. I could feel the smoothness of the wood railing as I drifted down the stairs, and when I took in a breath, I felt the air fill my lungs. I leaned against Darcy's back and noticed my heart pounding in my chest. She gasped, feeling it, too. When it was time to leave, panic set in. What if this was temporary? What if I was still trapped here?

I followed Darcy down the winding path to the driveway and made it right to the spot that had stopped me before. Except this time, I crossed over. Darcy's hand tightened in mine as we walked toward her car, trying not to run for fear that we'd wake up from this dream. We jumped in the car and Darcy started the engine. I felt the vibration beneath me and closed my eyes. As we drove away, realization completely set in.

"I think I'm alive," I said.

Her voice was breathy and filled with wonder. "I think you are, too."

A few days later, Mrs. Fitz called Darcy. As it turns out, Karen and Ralph eloped, and she no longer wanted the house. Mrs. Fitz knew that Darcy loved the house and thought she might like to buy it on the condition that Karen be allowed to visit her books and borrow from the library when she was in town. Of course, we readily agreed. We couldn't believe our luck. We still can't.

I have no explanation for what happened when we put on those rings, but neither one of us has ever or will ever take them off. Luna thinks we're soul mates and I would have to agree.

And now, as I stand here waiting for the love of my life to walk toward me, I'm overcome with emotion. This is our second chance after our first one was tragically ripped from us.

As the music continues and a voice sings about finding love where it wasn't supposed to be, the most breathtaking vision appears. Darcy drifts slowly toward me with her arm linked in her father's. It's almost as if her feet don't touch the ground as she seems to float closer. When they reach me, her father places a kiss on her forehead and shakes my hand.

And then it's just us and everything else becomes background noise.

She crinkles her nose adorably and whispers, "Hey, you."

"Hey," I whisper back. "You look amazing."

"You're not so bad yourself." Her lips curve. "So, since we're all dressed up, what do you say we get married again?"

I take her hands in mine. "I'd say there's nothing else I'd rather do."

We both lean in, and I mean for it to be a chaste kiss, but when I feel her lips part, I can't hold back. A throat clears, and we slowly break apart, acutely aware that we're on display in front of the whole town.

"We didn't get to that part yet, you two," Milly scolds, and the whole crowd erupts in laughter. Darcy's cheeks turn red.

"Sorry, I was just skipping to the good part. Can't blame a guy for trying, right?" I chuckle and I'm met with more laughter.

"Okay, well, if you're both ready, let's get you married," Milly announces.

The ceremony is short and timed perfectly with the setting sun. The warm golden light makes the garden appear like it's on fire. Darcy tells me she's been looking for me long before she even knew I existed. I rest a hand on her face, allowing my fingertips to glide into her hair. "I made you a promise and I'll make it again. I will love you in this life and every life hereafter. I once told you, you were my epilogue. But I was wrong. You're the whole damn book."

I don't wait for Milly's cue. Pulling Darcy close, I roll my forehead along hers. Our mouths collide in a dance that's slow and deliberate.

I will always wonder if I'm here on borrowed time. I was dead one day and alive again the next. Who's to say if any of this will last. But if I know one thing for certain, it's this: each day with Darcy is a gift. One that will be savored and never taken for granted.

I don't know how long I have, but our story isn't finished. It's filled with hundreds of blank chapters. It's time to start writing.

acknowledgments

My readers! I love each and every one of you. Thank you from the bottom of my heart for choosing to read my books. As a reader, I know how impossibly long our TBR's are and the fact that you made time for me is a huge honor.

To my incredible beta readers, Angela, Liz, and Marissa. Thank you for always dropping everything to read what I send you. Your feedback is everything. And special thanks to Marissa for the perfect title!

To Marla, thank you for making time for me and getting through this so quickly. I am forever grateful.

To Willow, thank you for encouraging me to write this book and give Vella a try. Your support means more than I can possibly put into words.

To my fellow author friends, you are all so amazingly supportive and I'm so happy to be a part of this indie community.

To Adam, every male character pales in comparison to you. Thank you for encouraging me to follow my dreams and making this life possible for me.

To my kiddos, Stella and Jasper, you are my favorite people. I am so proud of both of you and love you both so much.

Layne Deemer aims to push boundaries with her writing. Her stories deconstruct the ordinary until it becomes something else entirely.

She has a degree in Communications with a minor in English and has worked in the fields of public relations, marketing, and advertising, but writing has always been her true passion. When she isn't writing, she's reading. Her wish list of books will take her a lifetime to get through.

She resides in Pennsylvania with her husband, Adam, their two kids, Stella and Jasper, and their bulldog, Archie.

Other Books by Layne:
Frayed
Life Forgotten
Decompose
Under the Influence